DEEP FEAR

JETHRO WEGENER

SEVERED PRESS
HOBART TASMANIA

DEEP FEAR

1

The mini-submarine slid slowly through the eerie blackness of the underwater trench. On-board, two men sat, shivering slightly in the chill. One drank strong, black coffee from his thermos, using it to warm his hands. He was a skinny man, with long, wispy hair and a greying beard.

His partner, who was piloting the little sub, was a lot bigger—tall, with a large gut that strained against his shirt. He had long since lost the battle with male-pattern baldness, and his watery eyes strained to see something on the monitors in front of him that projected an image outside the sub.

"Bloody cold down here, isn't it, Roger?" asked the bearded man, taking another sip of his coffee.

"Jesus, Will, you say that every time," Roger replied in a bored tone. "We're miles away from the sun's lovely warmth, remember?"

"It bears repeating, my friend." The small submarine was heated, but the outside temperatures were so close to freezing that it seemed to make little difference.

Will had always hated deep dives in these tiny things. They were always uncomfortable, and the mysteries of the ocean had lost their allure to him when he was crammed into a tin can with another person like a sardine. It didn't help that Roger had been gaining weight at a steady pace since Lilith had left him two months prior. If the man didn't stop using food for comfort soon, he'd need the two-man sub all to himself.

"If you hate it so much, why don't you just quit?"

"And leave you here all alone? Nah, my friend," Will said, twisting the lid back on the thermos. "I'll retire when you do. Besides, we hardly dive that much anymore."

"Well, they usually don't need us. Until some idiot drops something down the bloody trench."

The two men hadn't been down in a few weeks, instead overseeing the construction from the relative comfort of the ship that was anchored far above their heads. The only reason they were diving now was because one of the workers had accidentally rolled a piece of building material down into the trench, with Roger and Will being the only two personnel available to go looking for it.

"Who the hell builds an underwater hotel so close to a bloody deep-sea trench anyway? More to the point, who the hell builds a hotel so far underwater?"

"Rich people, my friend."

"But it's so far underwater!"

"Their ways are alien to the likes of us."

Will chuckled. "And they always will be. When shall we head back up and tell them we can't find the bloody piece of pipe, or whatever the hell they dropped down here?"

"Jesus, Will, you're always griping. We've only been down," he checked his watch, "seventeen minutes."

Will looked at the camera feeds in front of him. They showed a barren sea floor, all life having scurried away from the harsh glare of the sub's headlamps. He turned his attention to the tiny porthole beside him, peering out into the inky blackness of the deep. It sent a chill down his spine every time. *Anything* could be out there, and the natural human fears of the unknown and the dark made a crappy cocktail.

"I mean, look at that," he complained. "Can't see a bloody thing. How do they expect us to find a goddamn—?"

His griping was cut short when the headlamps illuminated a piece of shiny metal, jutting out of the seabed at a forty-five-degree angle. Roger was already chuckling to himself.

"See? Patience, my moaning friend," he said, reaching for the radio. "Ahoy up there, Richie! We found your piece of piping."

"Thank fuck for that," Richie's voice came back through the sub's speakers, giving his voice an alien quality. "We got enough trouble without budget audits and questions from the damn environmentalists. Mark the location, we'll send someone down to pick it up."

"Roger that."

Will grinned. He always got a kick out of Roger saying stuff like that. However, his grin was soon replaced by a puzzled frown. He leaned forward in his seat.

"What is it?" Roger asked.

"You see that?" He pointed to something on the screen.

"What?"

"Looks like something moving. There! At the base of the pipe."

Roger leaned forward as well, struggling to pick out what his friend was seeing. He couldn't see anything at first, but then he did. Something seemed to be moving, *wriggling* around the base of the pipe.

"Get us closer, man," Will said, overcome by curiosity.

Nodding, Roger guided the little sub closer. For a reason he couldn't explain, his heart was pounding in his chest. Something wasn't right and his gut was churning furiously. Meanwhile, Will had his face as close to the screen as he could get it, trying to see what it was.

"It must be one of those underwater weirdos we always hear about," he was saying. "We could—"

Suddenly, the seabed went dark, cutting Will's sentence short. The submarine's floodlights had just cut off. Roger swore and started checking instruments, trying to find out what had just happened.

"The fuck just happened?" Will asked, a note of panic creeping into his voice.

"I don't fucking know." He reached for the radio. "Richie, come in, Richie! The lights just cut out. We're blind down here."

"Fuck," Richie said. "Get your asses back up here."

"Working on it."

Roger stopped fiddling and gripped the controls, getting ready to steer the submarine toward the surface. He activated the throttle, expecting movement. But instead, they held fast. Cursing, he increased speed. The sub jerked forward slightly and stopped, before it jolted backward, throwing both men forward in their seats.

Both Will and Roger smacked their heads into the bulkhead, causing both of them to see stars. Will leaned back, dazed and bleeding from a bad cut in his forehead. Roger tried to push himself back into his chair so that he could get them out of there. Suddenly, the walls started to groan, a low, threatening sound that chilled him to the bone.

"What the fuck was that?" Will asked, his words slurred slightly.

Roger was scrambling now, giving the throttle all that it had. The little sub didn't budge and the groaning intensified. He looked up and gasped in horror. The hull was being bent inward. They were being crushed like a soda can.

"Jesus Christ, Roger, get us out of here!" Will screamed.

"I'm fucking trying!" he yelled back.

A thought occurred to him. He stopped pushing forward and instead put the sub in reverse for a few seconds, before throttling forward again. It finally started moving forward and he almost laughed in relief.

"We might just make—" A terrible groaning sound cut his sentence short.

He looked at Will, who was peering out the porthole, trying to get some glimpse of whatever was behind them. Sweat pouring off of him, he gave it all he could, shooting through the water toward the surface. All they had to do was get into the light.

Suddenly, the submarine juddered, causing Roger to lose control. The groaning outside intensified, and the bulkhead started to cave inward again. He caught a glimpse of something passing across the porthole before the mini-submarine was crushed, he and Will along with it.

2

Six Months Later

Axel Calder shifted slowly and deliberately into a headstand position, keeping his breathing steady, the muscles on his lean body glistening with the sweat that he'd just worked up through his morning yoga routine. He usually ended his session with headstand meditation—it calmed his mind and rejuvenated his system better than any cup of coffee he'd ever tried.

Calder was six feet of lean muscle, with sandy blond hair, and a ruggedly handsome face. His short beard was neatly trimmed, and his hair cut short. An expertly done, intricately detailed black and grey tattoo of a scythe-wielding grim reaper riding a horse covered the entirety of his back.

A long scar ran diagonally across the left side of his chest, the result of a knife fight that had almost killed him as a teenager. There were a few other scars as well, the result of long stint in the SAS, and a few more brushes with death. It would have been obvious to any observer that the man was a warrior that was not to be messed with.

As he balanced, Calder let his mind go blank, focusing himself in the moment as he watched his breath enter and leave his body. His soul and emotions, which were always a mess after his nightmares, started to calm as he began to find his centre. The beginning of the day was always the hardest for him, but his morning routine, honed over many years, always worked to calm the battle inside himself.

After five minutes, he lowered himself down into child's pose for a moment, before shifting into corpse pose and letting his body go loose. He stayed there for a while, breathing slow and steady, before pushing up into a seated position, just as the noise of a small-engine plane reached his ears.

He glanced at the clock. It was about time for the last batch of visitors to arrive—a couple of reporters who had been called in to cover The Kingdom's grand opening, although they had an ulterior motive. He sighed as he stood up, because journalists had never been his favourite people. Then again, neither had unbelievably wealthy people, and he was about to be surrounded by those as well.

Calder grabbed his towel and went to shower. He'd have to be ready when Richie came to pick him up. As the head of security for the "biggest and best underwater hotel in the world," at least he wasn't going to spend that much time interacting with the guests, but he'd have to spend *some* time among them to make sure his team was doing their job correctly.

It took ten minutes for Calder to be showered and dressed in jeans and a white T-shirt. He was just pulling on his boots when he heard a jeep pull up outside and the horn sound. Calder yelled that he was coming, before sliding his Sig Sauer P226 pistol into his shoulder holster, grabbing his black rucksack, and heading out into the cloying jungle air.

Calder was situated in a small, nondescript, double-story building in the middle of a patch of green forest. A mud track ran up to the front of it, where a muddy clear served as a kind of carpark. He was on an island in the middle of the ocean which was acting as the stop-off for people wanting to go to The Kingdom. Visitors would fly in from their various destinations to the tiny island, and a luxurious yacht would take them to the hotel.

At the moment, the island was little more than a makeshift airport and muddy tracks, with one proper tarred road that ran from the airport to the jetty where the yacht was moored, but the person who had built the Kingdom with his own money—a man named Bernard Thompson—had big plans for the little island, including a Michelin-star restaurant and bar.

Thompson struck Calder as the kind of man who had big dreams about everything, and the money to make most of those dreams a reality—at least for a little while. Charismatic, charming, and a ruthless businessman, he had been smooth enough to get Axel on-board, and yet there was still something about the man that bothered him. That something had been bothering him even more since Will and Roger had disappeared and Thompson had given up the search.

Outside, Calder found a green, mud-splattered jeep waiting for him. Richie De Luca, head engineer, sat in the driver's seat, and two people sat in the back. One was a short, stocky man in his mid-forties, with grey hair that was shaved close to his scalp, a lined face, and black eyes. The other passenger was a dark-skinned, fit young woman with long, raven-black hair, and piercing almond eyes.

"Jones, Priya, meet Axel Calder, head of security for The Kingdom," Richie said as Calder climbed in beside him and shook hands with the other two.

Richie, a man in his early fifties with long, greying hair tied back in a ponytail, black eyes, and a bit of a belly straining against his thin linen shirt, reversed back onto the muddy track and started the drive toward the jetty.

"Pleasure," Calder said. "Jones your first or last name, mate?"

"Last," he said.

"I knew a Eugene Jones in Afghanistan, a journalist. He was embedded with one of our para units. You wouldn't be related to him, would you? Only you remind me of him."

Jones nodded. "He was my brother."

"I had the pleasure of spending some time with the man. I don't mind saying that I usually don't like journos, but your brother was an exception. I'm sorry about what happened. He was a hero."

"Thank you. Eugene wasn't supposed to be there."

"None of us were, mate," Calder said, noting that Priya seemed to be paying very close attention to the conversation. "Nothing we can do about it now. Richie, have you filled them in?"

He nodded. "I've given them the full brief. Their cover is that they're here to report on the grand opening, but they're actually trying to find out what Thompson is covering up about their disappearance."

"You trust them?" He glanced behind him. "No offence."

"None taken," Priya muttered.

"Jones and I have been friends for years, Axel. I trust him with my life."

"And Priya?" Calder asked.

"She's one of my best reporters," Jones said.

"And I know how to keep a secret, *mate*."

Richie chuckled. "Axel isn't the best at making friends. Comes with people in his line of work. He doesn't mean any harm."

"Also, keep in mind that both Richie and I are putting our jobs on the line here."

"Figures that a mercenary would only care about money," Priya shot back.

Calder laughed. "I'm no mercenary, luv, but I do need to eat."

"Will and Roger were *our* friends," Richie said. "It's not fucking right that Thompson just gave up looking."

"Why the grand opening if you suspect there's danger?" Priya asked.

"Because our benefactor is bleeding money. The man has a lot, but he also spends it like it's nothing. We're sure you've seen some of his experiments? He's a man of many grand ideas, but not all of them pay off. This opening is so that he can get the investors interested again and get the funds he needs to finish off the place."

"Hence why he's keeping the disappearances of the two workers so quiet?"

"Exactly," Calder said. "We can help you two get the evidence, you just have to be able to report it to everyone else. We need to use a softly-softly approach here. We get in, use the opening as a distraction to get the evidence to you two, and you get to splash it all over the headlines once it's all over. If Thompson finds out either Richie or I are involved, he can destroy us because of our contracts, but neither of us can sit back and let Will and Rog's families go without closure."

"Richie nodded. "Axel will be with you guys in the hotel, I'll be up top on the monitoring rig. I trust this man as much as I trust you, Jones. You can too."

"Did my brother trust you?" Jones asked.

Calder twisted in his seat to look him in the eye. "Your brother saved my life."

Jones nodded. "Okay."

"We're here," Richie said suddenly.

The jeep broke through the line of greenery and out onto an open field that faced the ocean. At least it would have, if there hadn't been a massive, gleaming white yacht obscuring their view. It was one of the biggest and most beautiful boats Priya had ever seen, and although she knew nothing about them, she could tell that this one was special.

It sat at the end of the pier, bobbing gently in the pale-blue water. People could be seen lounging on the decks, and the sounds of music and laughter drifted down toward the four in the jeep. The spectacle before her brought only two words to mind.

"Fuck me."

3

"She is an impressive sight. One of the largest privately owned yachts in the world," Calder said as he grabbed his pack and pulled himself out of his seat in one graceful movement. "Thompson already on-board, Richie?"

Richie was slightly less graceful getting out of the vehicle. "Everyone is. They're just waiting on us. Each of us has our own cabin."

"I'll bet they're a far cry from the ones given to the paying guests," Jones said.

"You'd be surprised."

Richie grunted as he pulled his bag out of the jeep before the four of them set off across the pier. As they walked, Priya watched Calder. The Englishman moved with an easy grace, carrying himself with confidence. She wasn't sure if she could trust him just yet, despite what Jones and Richie had said.

"It's impolite to stare, luv," Calder said.

"Just observing. I'm an investigative journalist—it's what I do."

"And what have you observed?"

"Not sure yet."

He laughed. "I'm not who you should be wary of. We're about to get on a yacht full of some of the richest people in the world. Those are the ones you should be watching."

They started up the steps leading to the deck, Richie going first, Jones second, Priya third, and Calder last. Priya missed a step halfway up and Calder steadied her with a hand on her shoulder.

"Thanks."

"No problem, luv."

Once they reached the deck, somebody in a pristine white uniform came over and started talking to Richie. He apologised, saying that he was needed, and that Calder would show them to their cabins before heading off with the crew member.

"This way."

They followed Calder through a side door, down a couple decks, and came to a corridor with doors to cabins on both sides. The floor was polished wood, the walls a pristine cream, and the railings and doors a classy polished wood. It was the richest setting Priya had ever set foot in, and she couldn't help feeling like she didn't belong.

Calder opened two doors that were across from one another. "Feel free to choose, they're both the same. I'm in the one at the end. If you need me, give me a shout, yeah?"

As Calder made his way to his cabin, Jones let Priya take the first pick. She chose the one on the left for no particular reason, and wasn't that surprised to find an amazing-looking room that included a comfortable-looking bed and on-suite bathroom. She ran her hand over the wood panelling and looked out the porthole at the expanse of pristine blue ocean. This was turning into a hell of an assignment.

The party could be heard happening overhead. It seemed to be in full swing, with people laughing raucously and music blaring. Priya pulled her camera from her bag and hung it around her neck. She needed to make it look like she was covering the opening.

Suddenly, she was struck with a pang of anxiety at the thought of all those people upstairs. Her heart rate quickened, and her breathing became erratic, causing her to hurry to the bathroom. She ran the tap, collected some of the water in her cupped hands, and splashed it over her face.

"Pull it together," she told her reflection.

She refused to have a full-on anxiety attack. When she's chosen to become a journalist, she knew that it would be difficult because she'd suffered from social anxiety all her life. But ever since she'd been a kid, she had wanted to write for a living, and nothing was going to stop her. With therapy, it had become a lot easier, but occasionally, when she was put in a whole new situation, her anxiety flared up again.

It probably had something to do with her being so out of place at the moment. Priya knew that the people on the yacht were from a completely different world, one that she would never be able to understand. She already felt like an outsider and was way out of her comfort zone.

She focused on her breathing for a moment, in through her nose and out through her mouth, slow and steady. After a while, her heart rate had calmed, and her breathing was back to normal. A knock on the door pulled her out of her meditation.

"We'd better get up there," came Jones' voice from outside her door.

"Coming," she said, and then stopped, looking down at herself.

Somehow, she didn't think that her jeans and T-shirt would cut it upstairs, so she asked Jones for five minutes and went scratching in her bag for more appropriate attire. Once she found it, she slipped out of her old clothes and into the new one, breathing a sigh of relief when she discovered that it still fit. After a couple squirts of perfume, she grabbed her camera again and opened the cabin door.

Jones had worked with Priya for over a year. In that time, she had proved to be an exceptionally talented journalist, as well as a damn good photographer, and he had never once really noticed what she looked like. That changed the moment she opened the door wearing a sheer black cocktail dress.

"I take it you like the dress?" Priya asked with a smirk.

"It's a mighty fine one. You look really good, if you don't mind me saying."

"Of course not. You don't look half bad yourself."

Jones had changed into chinos, a white shirt, and a light blue blazer. He could already feel the sweat starting to form on his back, but he wanted to look like he had made some sort of effort before he took the jacket off.

"Thank you. Let's go and mingle with the rich and powerful, shall we?" he said, offering his elbow.

They made their way to the upper deck where the party was happening. They arrived to find about twenty people dressed in a wide array of expensive clothing laughing, eating canapés, and drinking champagne. Waiters and waitresses, all young and good-looking, moved between the guests, clearing used glasses and plates, or taking drink orders. Deep house music played from overhead speakers.

Priya felt her heart rate quicken again. She felt ridiculously awkward, standing there in her heels and dress that must have cost less one of the branded handbags that a couple of the female guests were holding so nonchalantly. Money probably meant very little to these people.

Pull it together.

She took a deep breath and brought her camera up. The act of setting it up calmed her nerves, and by the time she had snapped her third picture, she felt more at ease. Jones watched her go before grabbing a glass of juice from one of the waiters and heading off to the side to lean on the railing.

Once there, he sipped at his orange juice and watched. He spotted Thompson almost immediately. The well-tailored, hellishly expensive cream-coloured suit made him stand out, even in his current company. He was a tall, fit, well-tanned man in his late fifties, with neatly combed and styled grey hair, black eyes, and a brilliant white smile.

He was going around shaking hands and having the odd conversation, obviously playing the perfect host. But Jones noticed that the smile seemed somewhat strained, bags were faintly visible under his eyes, and he moved like a man with a lot on his shoulders.

"That's Thompson," Richie said, appearing at Jones' side suddenly.

"I guessed. He looks tired."

"We all are. Wait here, I'll bring him over."

Richie moved off and attracted Thompson's attention. He said something, gestured to Jones, and brought the man over. Even though Jones was standing as tall as he possibly could, Thompson's six-foot-five-inch frame towered over him.

"Bernard Thompson," the man said, extending his hand and keeping his smile in place.

"Adam Jones."

They shook. The man's grip was firm, but his hands were soft, a sharp contrast to Jones' rough ones, hardened by years of wood work in his garage.

"Pleasure to meet you! Richie spoke very highly of you indeed, and I don't mind saying that's the reason I asked you to come along. But weren't there two of you?"

Jones pointed out Priya. "Priya Christie, my colleague."

Thompson whistled. "A fine young woman. Very fine. Now, I must get back to it. In about fifteen minutes, I'm going to give a short address covering where we're going how long it'll take us to get there, saying thanks, etcetera. If there are any questions or you require something, ask Richie, he'll see you get what you need. Oh, and tell your colleague to get my best side, okay?"

Another flash of brilliant white teeth and the man disappeared back into the crowd. Jones watched him go, wondering what to think of the man. One thing he knew for sure—he had not liked the look Thompson had given Priya. Not one bit.

4

Calder watched Thompson disappear back into the crowd from his spot near the railing three or so meters away from Jones. He'd been alternating between scanning the crowd and the ocean since he had come up on deck, keeping alert. There had been a couple reports of pirates in the area, and he wasn't taking any chances.

Something was making him uneasy, and it wasn't just the missing men, or the fact that he was basically betraying his boss. It was something else, the same feeling he'd had all those years ago when things went tits up in Afghanistan. Soldiers had an almost sixth sense sometimes, and his was going into overdrive. At least the weight of the Sig in its shoulder holster was giving him comfort.

"All good, Axel?"

"Not really," Calder said, turning to face the man who had just come up behind him.

Ekkow Afolami nodded. He was a big man with dark skin, a bald head, and muscles that seemed to strain against his suit. His brown eyes scanned the crowd and the horizon before coming back to Calder.

"So, you're getting the same feeling I am then?" Ekkow asked.

"Pretty much. It doesn't help that Eugene's brother is here."

"You're shitting me?"

Calder shook his head and pointed to Jones. "That one over there."

"Even looks like him. Now that brings back all kinds of bad memories."

"Mine never went away."

Ekkow put a massive hand on Calder's shoulder and squeezed. "I know, bruv. His brother know what happened?"

"Classified op. He can't know."

"I thought you would have given him something."

"What good would it do, mate? His brother is still dead. It was still my fault."

"Might help you."

Calder laughed. "Nah, mate, I get on just fine."

"Don't we all, bruv? I miss Eugene though. Only journo who I was happy to babysit."

"He was one funny fucker. Looks like he got the sense of humour though."

"Dour one, is he? Looks like I'll have to provide all the laughs on this one then."

"Mate, you're about as funny as May is."

Ekkow's face broke out in a display of mock hurt and he clutched at his heart. "You got me right in the heart with that one, bruv."

Calder laughed. "I just want to shake this feeling."

"Well, if we get in the shit, at least you know I've got your back, and our lads aren't too bad either."

"You two expecting trouble then?" Priya asked, coming out of the crowd to stand in front of the two men.

Ekkow's face broke out in the biggest smile and he extended his hand. "I see Axel has been holding out on me, the rude fucker. My name is Ekkow."

Priya took the offered hand and shook. "Priya. I work with Jones. A journo, I guess you'd say? You part of the security team?"

"I'd say I'm *the* security team. Axel and the others are just there for show."

"I feel safer already," Priya said with a laugh. "I'm assuming you both served in the same unit?"

Calder nodded. "Both part of the Regiment."

"Regiment?"

"SAS, luv," Ekkow replied. "Axel and I were honoured to be part of the greatest special forces unit in the world."

"I love your humility."

"Everyone does. I'm told it's my second-best feature."

"And what's the first?"

"Wouldn't you like to know?" Ekkow said with a wink. "Now, I'm sorry to be rude, but I need to go and make sure our team has the bodyguards squared away. It's been a pleasure."

Calder and Priya watched Ekkow go below deck, and stood in awkward silence for a moment. It was Priya who spoke first.

"So, you knew Jones' brother?"

"He was embedded in our unit for a while."

"Jones never talks about him, you know."

"People deal with loss in different ways."

She studied his face before nodding. "I guess so. Anyway, I have to get back to work. Later."

Calder nodded and watched her head off, snapping photos as she went.

"Well," he said to himself, "that went well, didn't it, dickhead?"

5

"Why the fuck am I always the one doing the dirty work?" Billy asked himself in the darkness.

He was slowly making his way down one of The Kingdom's many service tunnels. The network of pipes and cables that ran across the ceiling and walls was making his progress harder. Valves, knobs, and various protruding pieces were everywhere, forming an intricate web of metal, and he was already bent double to fit his six-foot frame into the tiny space. It was a good thing he was about the width of a chopstick, as his dad used to say.

"What was that?" came a voice over the radio clipped to his shoulder.

"I said, why the fuck am I always the one going into these tunnels?"

"Because you're smaller than I am."

"Bullshit, George, you're half my height."

"But twice your width in muscle, Billy. Now stop moaning. How far away are you?"

Billy checked the map on his tablet PC. "Not far. But, dude, what the hell is wrong this time?"

"I dunno, man. Blocked pipe or something. System is just giving me a blockage warning, and we have to get it fixed fast. The boss is on his way as we speak."

"Fuck this. This place isn't ready to be open."

"Well, do you want to keep getting paid? If so, then we need those rich fuckers to come spend their money."

Billy sighed. George had a point. Even he, as low down on the totem pole as he was, had heard the rumours that the boss was running out of cash.

"Now stop moaning and clear the channel until you get there. Out."

George clicked off, leaving Billy alone once more. He pulled his parka around himself as his teeth started chattering. All around him was the steady drip of water as the condensation that formed on the pipes fell to the floor. He was walking in one great big puddle, thankful his boots were waterproof. Wet feet would have just soured his mood even more.

He swore loudly as his head caught on a particularly nasty protruding bit of pipe. He gingerly touched the spot with his fingers and they came away slick with blood. More swear words followed as he pulled his handkerchief out of his jacket pocket and pressed it against the wound.

"Just what I need," he muttered to himself. "Cold, wet, and now in pain. I do so love my job."

His tablet made a sound, indicating that he was at the site of the blockage, and he stopped. He shone his flashlight over the various pipes around him, looking for the one that was blocked. It didn't take him long to find it.

"What the actual fuck?"

A thick, glistening lump of black gunk clung wetly to one of the pipes. It seemed to be moving, writhing under the glare of the flashlight, but Billy put it down to a trick of the light. As he watched, the gunk seemed to expand, becoming bigger and covering more of the pipe, slowly, as if someone was slowly squeezing it out like toothpaste from a tube.

"George, come in."

"Yeah, what is it?"

"It looks like there's something coming out of the pipe."

"Huh?"

"There's some kind of black goop coming out of the pipe here. Looks gnarly."

"Take a picture and send it to me."

Billy pulled up the camera on his phone and snapped a picture. He was temporarily blinded as the flash went off. He blinked his eyes repeatedly and could have sworn that the goop had moved when the flash went off. It had to be another trick of the light.

"Sent."

"Jesus," George exclaimed. "What the fuck is that?"

"This pipe leads out into the ocean, right?"

"Yeah, it's one of the waste pipes."

"You think this came from out there?"

"Christ, I hope not. That's all we need is gunk in our systems. Hang on, I'm going to try and flush the pipe. I want you tell me what happens."

As Billy waited, he gazed at the black stuff. A shudder ran through him as it occurred to him how far down he was. Tons of water were kept at bay by a thin metal skin—the only thing between him and an agonising death. On the one hand, it was an engineering marvel; on the other, he was wondering why the fuck the place had ever been built.

"Okay, I'm going to start low, and then slowly increase the pressure. Tell me if it has any effect."

Billy watched as George relayed the amount of pressure he was using to flush the pipe over the radio. At first, there was very little effect, but then the goop started to tremble slightly. It took about 30 seconds for it to start receding into the pipe once more.

It slid slowly, leaving a thin, sickly trail of grey in its wake. It looked like it was fighting against the pressure, trying its best to stay out of the pipe.

"It looks to be—" Billy's sentence was cut off as the black goop exploded out toward him, covering his face in slime.

He jumped back, coughing and spluttering, and banged into the pipes behind him. An intense pain shot up his spine as a protruding valve caught him in the middle of his back. He cried out, still trying frantically to wipe the goop off of his face. It felt like it was moving over him, looking for a way inside, and before he knew it, the stuff was *flowing* into him.

It poured into his nose, the open wound on his forehead, and his mouth as he opened it to scream. No sound came from his lips as the black gunk flowed down his throat, choking him. He felt it forcing its way into his stomach, expanding his oesophagus on the way down. As it flowed into the wound in his head, it stretched the skin, so it looked like someone was pumping water between his skull and flesh.

Billy fell to the floor, writhing in pain, clawing at his throat. In his agony, he prayed for death, or any kind of release from what was happening, but somehow, he could still breathe, as if the stuff was keeping him alive.

Then, as suddenly as it had begun, it was over. He was left curled up in a foetal position on the wet floor, able to breathe normally again, and the pain dissipated. There was no light, as the flashlight had been broken in the struggle, leaving Billy to sob in the darkness, with only the sound of dripping water and George's frantic shouts coming from the radio to keep him company.

6

Two members of the maintenance crew were dispatched to Billy's last known location as soon as communication with him was lost. They found him still curled up on the floor, complaining about how much his head hurt, mumbling incoherent gibberish. The two men radioed for a medical team, who arrived swiftly and carted the man off to sick bay.

The Kingdom's resident doctor, Henry Goldstein, could find nothing wrong with the man, save for the bump on his head, and could not make any sense out of his gabbling. At one point, Billy started screaming and had to be sedated, after which the doctor decided that it was time Thompson heard about what was going on.

"…and that's all we've been told," Calder concluded, sitting back down in the plush leather chair.

He, Ekkow, Thompson, Richie, and one of Thompson's PR men were gathered around a large mahogany table in the yacht's meeting room. Calder had been the first one informed once the doctor had radioed the yacht, and it was he who had called the meeting. Thompson did not look pleased.

"So, the doctor can't find anything wrong?" he asked, while he fiddled with his expensive, gold cuff-links. "What's his theory?"

"He doesn't have anything solid."

"Come on, Axel, the guy must have given you something because there's no way you didn't push. I know you better than that."

Calder sighed. "Well, since the only sign of injury appears to be the head wound, the doc is thinking it possible that a mental break brought on by being down so far for too long. However, he stressed that that's just one of many possible solutions. Personally, I think Goldstein is just taking shots in the dark."

"Fuck," said the PR guy. "That could mean a massive lawsuit if this gets out."

Ekkow and Calder exchanged a look but remained quiet. They had to pick their battles and decided to wait until Thompson spoke again. The older man was still playing with his cuff-links absentmindedly.

"I want to hear your advice, Axel."

"Well, taken alone, this incident doesn't mean much. However, when we take into account what happened to the submarine crew, I have reason to believe that the security of The Kingdom is compromised in some way. I would suggest a shutdown of the hotel until we can do a thorough security check."

"Not possible. I cannot ask the people on this boat to head back home, not after they have travelled so far and spent so much. I need you and Ekkow to find a way to do the security check without alerting the guests. And I want you," he added, turning to the PR guy, "to come up with a plan in case this leaks. I cannot afford the bad press. If I have to pay the guy a shit ton, I will, as long as this incident doesn't get out, you understand me?"

The PR guy nodded. Ekkow gave Calder another look.

"With all due respect," Ekkow said, standing up and placing his hands on the table, "Axel just told you what is the best course of action, Mr. Thompson. It would be in your best interests to listen to the man who you pay to look after you, your pet project, and perhaps most importantly for your fucking bottom line, your important guests."

Thompson didn't say anything for a moment. He just looked up at Ekkow, making sure to maintain eye contact with the big man, before slowly turning to Calder.

"Tensions are high at the moment," he said slowly, "so I'll forgive that outburst. But the bottom line is this—I pay your salaries. I am your boss. You will listen to me because you need The Kingdom to be a hit as much as I do. So, what I want you to do is find a way to make sure my guests are safe *without* them knowing that there's anything amiss, am I clear?"

Calder stood and put his hand on Ekkow's shoulder, pushing him gently back into his seat. He nodded to Thompson, and then sat back down as well. The PR guy was on his phone, oblivious to his surroundings as he worked to figure out the best possible plan of action.

"Good," Thompson said and flashed his brilliant white teeth, "then that's settled. Thank you, gentlemen. Now, if you'll excuse me, I have a party to attend."

He rose, straightened his suit, squared his shoulders, and strode out of the meeting room with the PR guy following close behind.

"Fucking cunt," Ekkow said. "Only thing that guy cares about is his bottom line. How the fuck does he expect us to ensure the safety of his guests?"

"He expects us to find a way, mate, so let's do just that. Our mission is to make sure no one else gets hurt, and when we get back to land, we let the journos do their job. Until then, we do our jobs, just like always. Just a little longer."

7

Billy was in agony. He felt like there were hundreds of tiny insects crawling beneath his scalp, worming their way across the bone under his skin. He felt like he could actually see the pain in front of his eyes—black splotches that danced across his vision. Tears streamed from his eyes, snot ran out his nose. He was aware of other people in the room, but only vaguely. The pain was overriding everything else.

"Stop him screaming!" George said from the corner of the room, chewing on his thumb.

Two orderlies were trying desperately to hold Billy down while Doctor Goldstein scrambled for the sedative. Billy was thrashing and kicking. His right foot caught one orderly in the face, smashing his nose, causing him to spurt blood all over the white, linoleum floor.

The second orderly's shoes slipped in the blood and he toppled over backward, only just managing to catch himself before he cracked his head on the counter behind him.

"Help me!" the man growled, pulling George over to the thrashing Billy. "Hold him the fuck down!"

George was wide-eyed with fear but did as he was told. He leaned all his weight on Billy's left side, the muscles in his arms straining. For a skinny guy, Billy seemed to have all the strength in the world.

"Any minute now, doc!" the orderly yelled.

Goldstein finally filled the needle with the right dosage and rushed back to the gurney, stepping over the injured man on his way. He instructed George to hold Billy's arm steady before plunging the needle into it.

"Just hold him while we wait for it to take effect," the doctor said, throwing the needle into the corner of the room and joining in the effort to hold Billy down.

It took a few minutes, but finally Billy started to settle. Eventually, he stopped thrashing around and went still. George collapsed to the floor, breathing heavily, while Goldstein attended to the injured orderly.

"Christ on a bike," said the other man, whose name tag read Frank, wiping sweat from his brow, "how the hell did he manage to fight us for so long?"

"Patients going through a mental breakdown can be incredibly strong," Goldstein said. He was examining the second guy's broken nose, prodding it gently with his fingers. "Even though I'm not qualified to speculate, I'd say being down here for so long has taken a serious mental toll on Billy."

"He seemed fine to me," said an exhausted George. "Same jokey, swearing guy he's always been."

"Well, some of these guys can hide it really well," Frank said. "I remember working in a psych ward back in Philly. You could have sworn some of them didn't have any issues up there whatsoever. But, man, when they snapped, they went all kinds of crazy."

"I don't like that word, Frank," Goldstein said. "Now, if you could please help me restrain Billy for his own safety, while I attend to John, that would be much appreciated."

Half an hour later, George and Goldstein were seated in Goldstein's office, sipping on whiskey-spiked coffee. The doctor had already reported the latest incident to Calder. Open in his lap was the Diagnostic and Statistical Manual of Mental Disorders, which was the book that listed the common criteria and traits of known mental illnesses.

"Why don't you just Google it?" George asked. He had watched the doctor slowly page through the book for the past ten minutes.

"Because I prefer physical books, my boy."

"But it takes so long to find things."

"It calms me down. And after that commotion, I need it."

"This is what calms me, doc," George said, holding up the mug before taking a sip.

"Oh, this helps too, believe me. But back to your friend in sickbay, are you sure he hasn't been acting differently lately?"

George shook his head. "Not at all. There have been no massive changes in his life, no changes in his mood, nothing. He's just been the same as always. I'm pretty sure he doesn't have any previous mental health issues."

"Hmm. Then maybe something to do with his head wound?" Goldstein let out an exasperated sigh. "I don't know, and I don't have the equipment to find out down here."

"Can we evacuate him? Get him to the surface?"

"Not in his current state. We can't risk it. We'll see how he is when he comes around again. We just have to hope whatever this is subsides long enough for us to get him up top."

"Goddamn it. This is the worst job we've ever taken, I swear to God. You sure this is mental?"

The doctor sighed. "No, I'm not. I only told Calder that was a possible, because physically he seems fine. But there are so many possible explanations, almost none of which I can accurately test for down here. Can't do scans or tests or anything. So I'm going to do the only things I can do."

"Which are?"

"Keep Billy as comfortable as possible while I go through every textbook I have to try and find a possible solution."

"Will you?"

Goldstein laughed. "Not this way. This isn't a movie where we will stumble across the most likely solution by accident. But it'll keep *me* from losing my mind because I'll feel like I'm doing something, even though there really is nothing I can do."

"Doctor!" came Frank's panicked voice from the infirmary. "Something's happening!"

Goldstein and George rushed to the other room, almost dropping their cups in their haste. They arrived to see Frank standing with his back pressed up against the wall, an expression of sheer terror on his face. Their eyes were drawn to Billy on the table.

He lay still, but there was something *coming out of him*. Some kind of black gunk was leaking out of every orifice—his ears, eyes, nose, mouth, and even his pants were soiled by it. It came out slowly, oozing out of the patient, more viscous than blood or mucous.

"What the fuck is that?" George breathed.

Goldstein didn't say anything as he rushed to one of the cupboards that lined the wall. He pulled out a pair of rubber gloves and snapped them on before grabbing a plastic container, the kind usually reserved for piss samples, and a wooden tongue depressor.

"Let's see if we can find out," he said, stepping up to the gurney and pressing the beaker just under Billy's ear.

He used the depressor to scrape some of the black stuff into it, before stepping back and screwing the beaker shut. He held the thing up to the light to examine it.

"Jesus fucking Christ," Frank said. "It's still coming out of him. What do we do?"

"Don't touch it," Goldstein said, staring in horrified fascination as the stuff leaked out of the unconscious man. "We're putting him and ourselves under quarantine. This isn't a mental illness—it's something else entirely."

George was shaking, unable to take his eyes off of his friend. "I repeat—worst fucking job ever."

8

"The four of us are going to go into quarantine," came Goldstein's voice over the radio. "I wouldn't advise bringing anyone else into The Kingdom."

"Is it a confirmed contagion?" Thompson asked.

He was alone in the yacht's radio room. As soon as the call had come in, Thompson had known it would be bad. He'd immediately had the room cleared. The doctor had just filled him in on the latest development.

"No, but…"

"Is it contained?" Thompson said, cutting him off.

"For now, it appears to—"

"Then keep it that way. I cannot turn this yacht around—not when we're only an hour away. We'll keep the guests out of the sections near the medical bay and the tunnel where the man was infected or whatever, but we are not turning around."

"Mr. Thompson, with all due respect, I cannot let you bring guests down here at this time."

"I repeat, do you suspect this to be a contagion?"

"I do not know what it is, if I'm honest. I'm not thinking it's an infectious disease yet, because it doesn't look like any that I know of."

"So, the quarantine is the safety measure you have implemented to keep the hotel safe, is that correct?"

"Yes, it is, but—"

"Listen, Goldstein, I pay your salary, and you all signed the contracts. Two things on said contracts that I'd like you to remember right now are these—I have the final word, and the nondisclosure agreements. I'm confident there is no danger to my guests since it is contained."

"I'd like it known for the record that I advised against this."

"This whole conversation is on tape," Thompson lied, "and you will be well compensated for your trouble."

There was a silence for a moment. "How well?"

Thompson quoted a number and heard the intake of breath from the doctor. He allowed himself a small grin—any business deal that ended with both parties happy was a good one.

"I'll implement quarantine procedures immediately and keep you advised of any developments, Mr. Thompson."

"And one other thing—this remains between us, understood?"

"Understood."

"I knew I could count on you, doctor," Thompson replied, severing the connection.

He reached under his expensive shirt and gripped the small silver crucifix that hung around his neck. After a small prayer that there would be no more trouble, he composed himself before leaving the radio room. He hoped God was listening, because he needed His help at the moment.

"Everything all right?" Calder asked, coming around the corner. "You look distressed."

"I'm worried about the maintenance man. I was just trying to get hold of his family."

"Oh? I thought your PR team would have done that."

"I'm not a heartless bastard, Axel. I'm offended that you'd think that."

Calder studied him for a moment. "I'm sorry. It's been a long day."

"It's alright. I know what you mean. But all we have to do is make sure this opening goes well, then it's all going to settle down. I'm going to pay you all very well for the loyalty you've shown me."

"And the men who've been hurt?" It came out before he could stop himself.

"I promise to do what I can for them and their families. And I know I can count on you to make sure no one else gets hurt. Now, I must go upstairs and play the gracious host. We are about an hour away from The Kingdom; I trust you know what to do?" Calder nodded. "Excellent."

Calder watched as Thompson strode off, unable to shake the feeling that he'd just heard a lot of empty words that held no truth behind them.

***

Priya sighed, sitting down heavily in one of the many chairs that were scattered around the dining tables. She'd been taking photos for what seemed like hours, while also mingling as best she could. The rich and famous had hit on her about twenty separate times—including offers of diamonds from one man who said she had looked exotic, like a princess from Arabia, apparently. It had taken all her willpower not to snort in his face.

"Bored, huh?"

Priya looked to her side to see a young Chinese girl seated beside her. She had raven-black hair pulled back into a tight ponytail, dark eyes that were obscured by round-rimmed glasses, and flawless skin. Her outfit was incredibly basic compared to the rest of the guests—a simple white T-shirt and ripped skinny jeans, completed with black Doc Martens.

"How did you guess?"

"The world-weary sigh that you gave as you sat down. Plus, the fact that you basically fell into that chair."

"Observant."

"I try to be. I'm Anna, by the way."

"Priya."

"Reporter, right? Since you've been taking photos all this time, you're either that or just really interested in the dynamics of dull parties."

"You've been watching me?"

"Pretty much. These things are always so damn boring, so whenever something different happens, it attracts attention. I'd say a pretty lady taking pictures of everyone is different. Usually the photographers they send aren't the greatest lookers."

Priya laughed. "Well, I think you're onto something there—I feel like I've been hit on by every man in this place. While they were next to their wives, no less."

Anna grimaced. "To be honest, I think the wives expect it by this point. They get the money, side chick gets the terrible sex. That's not me speaking from experience, by the way, just a guess."

A snort of laughter escaped Priya's lips before she could stop it. She felt herself start to blush.

"By the way, not that I think you can't take care of yourself or anything, but stick with me if you don't want to be perved on. These guys wouldn't dream of pissing off my dad."

"Should I be worried?"

"You? Never. But he'd have a fit if someone tried it with me."

"Who is he? If you don't mind me asking."

"You won't have heard of him, since you don't move in these circles. These guys know him though. He's one of the richest men in Singapore—and that's really saying something."

"Sounds like an interesting person to be raised by."

"Oh, you have no idea. He's very traditional Chinese-Singaporean. He wants me to be the proper daughter, which I failed at."

"I know that feeling. Asian kid problems," Priya said with a chuckle. "So, you're from Singapore? That's cool. I was trying to place the accent."

"Yep. Contrary to popular belief, it is not located in China."

"I wasn't even aware that people thought that."

"The number of times I've had people tell me that my English is very good. It's fucking infuriating. Yes, we speak English as our first language over there! It's my Chinese that's terrible!"

Priya was about to reply when she heard Thompson calling for attention. She and Anna looked up to see him at the other end of the deck, beaming.

"Ladies and gentlemen, we are about to arrive at our last stop before we reach The Kingdom proper. I invite you all to collect your luggage and get ready to leave the yacht!"

Priya saw a structure that jutted out of the ocean. It resembled one of those offshore oil rigs—a platform suspended above the water on sturdy-looking stilts, except a lot less industrial looking. However, it was no less bizarre and unnatural, a mix of polished glass windows, concrete, and steel.

As the boat drew nearer to the rig, Priya felt the anxiousness start to get to her. It dawned on her exactly where she was going. Far down into the dark depths, an inhospitable place that humans were never meant to reach. The thought was at once thrilling and terrifying, and she didn't know which emotion was more prevalent.

9

As soon as Billy had started leaking black fluid, Goldstein had implemented quarantine procedures. The medical bay and the room Billy was in had been sealed, the biohazard suits had been broken out of storage, and the rest of the hotel had been warned to keep away. The doctor also radioed up to the monitoring rig to let them know what was happening. The only thing he hadn't done was tell them the whole truth.

"It's all just a precaution. The patient is displaying some odd symptoms, and I want to be sure that he isn't infectious. Nothing to worry about."

It wasn't the first time Goldstein had lied, and it wouldn't be the last, but it was the first time that he was having to battle his conscience over it. The money was helping though—enough that he could finally retire and stop having to spend every day of his life worrying about other people.

"Are you sure we're okay, doc?" Frank asked nervously, his clothes soaked with nervous sweat.

"We're fine. None of us had any physical contact with the substance, and I'm certain we're not dealing with an infectious disease. Just try and relax—it'll be over before you know it."

"So, what do we do until then?" George asked.

The doctor picked up the sealed jar of the substance that he had taken. "I need to examine this as much as I can. The sooner I discover what this is, the sooner we can all go back to our lives. Such as they are down here anyway."

***

Meanwhile, in the medical bay, Billy was twitching. It wasn't conscious movement, as he was still out cold, but rather something was moving him. Underneath his skin, things moved, causing it to undulate in unnatural ways. The fluid still leaked from his ears, nose, mouth, and eyes, but only minute traces, as if it did not want to leave the body anymore.

Suddenly, Billy started to spasm, his limbs thrashing violently, his breathing becoming ragged and harsh. He twisted and yanked, and there was a sickening snap as his neck bent at an odd angle, but he did not stop moving for a full minute, until finally, he settled.

His chest continued to rise and fall, his eyes moved behind closed eyelids, and his fingers twitched intermittently. If someone had been watching him closely, they would also have seen the black fluid flowing back into him, slowly, working its way back into his body.

Soon, all of it had flowed back into the unconscious man. A second later, his twitching stopped and he lay still for a moment. His breathing stopped—but only for a minute—then his eyes popped open and he gasped, drawing air deep into his lungs.

Billy blinked in the harsh light of sick bay. He felt different somehow, wrong in a way he couldn't quite place. Better, for sure, but there was something that was off. It scared him.

The man lay still for a while, doing a mental check of his body. He started by twitching his toes and moved up from there. Everything seemed to be working. His breathing was normal, if a little laboured. Physically, he seemed fine, except for a slight headache.

He reached up and touched the wound on his forehead. It was barely a scratch, which was odd because he seemed to remember it being a lot worse. Then again, he realised that he didn't remember very much.

All he could recall were bits and pieces. Vague memories of being in the maintenance tunnels, a blockage, black gunk, and pain. Excruciating pain. But that was gone now, although there was something else in its place.

Billy swung his feet off the edge of the gurney and sat up. His head swam a bit, his vision blurring slightly. After a couple of deep breaths, it settled. The room stopped spinning, and he risked standing up.

The tiled floor was freezing cold against his bare feet. He realised just then that he was shivering slightly. At some point, they'd taken off his clothes and dressed him in a hospital gown.

He had an urge to call out, to ask for help, but something was stopping him. It was like there was something influencing his decisions, but of course that was ridiculous. He was fine. He felt fine. Didn't he?

The answer that occurred to him was simple. No. He wasn't. Something was seriously wrong, and it was scaring him. It scared him more that he couldn't quite put his finger on what it was. He felt a tear roll down his cheek. His instincts were telling him to call for help, to scream for it, but he couldn't.

Billy felt trapped, even though he wasn't. It was like he didn't quite have full control. He raised his hand to his face. It did as he wanted. He made a fist, and his index finger remained straight. He tried again, but the result was the same.

As he struggled to curl his index finger inward, something else happened. To his horror, his other fingers started to unfurl themselves, starting with his thumb. There was excruciating pain as it happened, his muscles fighting against what was being done, his brain struggling to do what he wanted, but it was no use.

Billy watched, unable to cry or call out, as his hand took on a life of its own, clenching and opening a few more times before stopping. His skin rippled, as if hundreds of tiny bugs were crawling beneath it. He stared open-mouthed at it, unable to fully comprehend what was happening. Something had just taken control of his hand.

Then it stopped, as suddenly as it had begun. He had control of his hand again, and this time he was able to make a fist. He clenched it as hard as he could for a moment, before he threw up all over the floor.

Black gunk poured out of his mouth, the viscous liquid pooling at his feet. He continued to wretch, his body wracking each time, the pain in his throat almost unbearable. It felt like the black goo was forcing its way up his throat, desperate to get out.

Finally, it stopped, and Billy fell backward, hitting the floor with a dull thump. His head bounced off the steel surface, causing him to see stars. He was vaguely aware that the door to the room had opened. There was someone in the room.

Frank had watched Billy puke, as well as saw him fall. He hurriedly slipped into a hazard suit and entered the room, closing the door behind him. He winced when the door sealed with a metallic thunk as his heart beat harder in his chest.

"Billy?" Frank asked, moving forward slowly, gingerly avoiding the black gunk that was spreading across the floor.

Billy lifted his hand up toward Frank. He groaned as his body twitched.

"It's going to be okay, man. Let me just get you back up on the bed."

As Frank moved toward Billy, he could have sworn the stuff on the floor was reacting to his movements. But that was crazy, wasn't it?

Dismissing the thoughts from his mind, Frank reached down and grasped Billy's hand. That's when Billy's other hand moved.

It shot out and grabbed the hazard suit at Frank's leg, before pulling back. There was a dreadful tearing sound that made Frank's blood run cold. He looked down to a see that his suit's integrity was severely compromised.

"How the hell…?" He asked in disbelief, wondering how the man had had the strength to tear his suit. But then he noticed the black goop. It was moving up his leg. "Jesus fucking Christ."

Frank tried to leap backward, but his leg was stuck to the floor, held solid by the black stuff that was heading toward the rip in his suit. He tried to scrape it off with his hands, but all that happened was that his hands got stuck to his leg.

The stuff was moving faster and faster, flowing into the tear. He could feel it against his skin, soft, slimy, and freezing cold. He tried to scream but couldn't manage it. Soon the stuff was flowing into his body. It went through every opening it could find.

Frank jittered and twitched as the stuff flooded into him. As he looked up to let out a silent scream of horror, the gunk filled up his eyes, turning them an inky black.

10

"As soon as we get down there, I want you to head to the medical bay," Calder said. "Something doesn't feel right."

Ekkow nodded. "I've got the same feeling, bruv."

"Take one of our guys with you. Someone you trust."

"Gotcha."

Ekkow hurried off, grabbing a man on the way. Calder turned and looked out to sea. They were on the rig, all the guests were getting ready to board the subs, and the ocean looked peaceful. Yet Calder couldn't shake the feeling that something was up.

He peered down into the water, wishing he could see all the way down to The Kingdom. The last ten minutes of his life had been wasted arguing with Thompson about postponing the launch. It had all culminated in the rich arsehole threatening to fire him if he kept pushing. Which would have meant that Calder wouldn't be going down, and he felt he'd be needed down there.

The weight of the Sig in its holster gave him some comfort, but he hoped he wouldn't need it. If it was a biological problem down there, there was nothing the weapon could do anyway. Unless the threat happened to be zombies.

He chuckled at the thought. The chuckle turned into a nostalgic smile as he remembered the time he and his little sister had stayed up late to watch a movie they weren't supposed to— Night of the Living Dead, the original '60s version. He'd had nightmares for weeks afterward. His sister, on the other hand, had made the smart choice and hidden behind the couch the whole time.

"What's so funny, soldier?" Priya asked, coming up behind him, with a Chinese girl in tow.

"Old memories." He extended his hand to the young lady. "Axel Calder."

"Anna," the girl said. "So, you're security, huh?"

She had clocked the gun.

"Not just security," Priya said. "He's *Head* of Security. This man's job is to keep us safe down there."

"I'm impressed," Anna said, somewhat sarcastically. "Bet that sidearm will come in really handy against all those weird fish."

Calder laughed. "A job by any other name. How's the picture taking coming along?"

"Splendidly, thanks," Priya replied, snapping a quick picture of him. "I've never seen so many glamorous people in all my life."

"You get used to it. Hanging out with Thompson has given me ample chance to do so."

"You see?" Anna said, playfully slapping Priya's shoulder, then quickly shoving her hands in her pockets and stumbling over the next few words. "I told you that you would."

"Priya, can I talk to you for a moment?" Calder asked, motioning her away.

"Sure. Give me a moment, will you please, Anna?"

"No problem. I'll go and get my stuff ready for the sub. Later."

"What is it?" Priya asked, once Anna was out of earshot.

"There's something going on down there. A man was injured, and Thompson wants this launch to go through, despite my objections."

"Your gut is telling you something is wrong, isn't it?"

"Yes, luv. So I want you and Jones to be careful down there. If shit goes down, you stick with my men and me. We'll keep you safe."

"What are you worried about exactly? You're talking like there's going to be some kind of attack."

"You ever get the feeling that something is very wrong, and you can't quite put your finger on why? Like the world is slowly coming to an end and you're the only burke who hasn't noticed yet."

"Maybe."

"Well, that's how I feel right now. And I felt something similar on the day Jones' brother was killed. I wasn't prepared for shit to hit that fan then, but I sure as hell will be today."

Priya studied his face. The hard lines, the piercing eyes, the seriousness and pain that lived behind them.

"Okay. I'll tell Jones."

"Good. And keep that young girl close to you. I'm not having another child's death on my conscience."

Priya caught herself before she asked the obvious question—*another?*—and instead nodded and hurried off.

"Ekkow? One more thing," Calder said, keying his radio.

"Yes, boss?"

"I want the heavy ordnance on this one, you get me, mate?"

"Loud and clear, boss."

Calder turned and stared out across the ocean, watching it rise and fall rhythmically. Those dark waters were hiding something, he was sure of it. The sick, empty pit in his stomach told him so.

The only question was—what the hell was it?

***

Jones stared at the mini-subs that were going to ferry them to The Kingdom. He was feeling slightly queasy just looking at the cramped little things. Thompson had to be crazy to think that people would pay for this. A shrill laugh behind him almost instantly proved how wrong he was.

Tight spaces had never been his thing. Hell, the only reason he'd volunteered for this job was Richie. But he was already shitting himself at the thought of being under all that water in cramped quarters.

"She's a beauty, ain't she?" Richie said.

"That's one word for it, I guess."

"I love these things. State of the art, first class tech. One thing about Thompson, he doesn't skimp where it counts. Mostly anyway."

"You don't know me very well, do you, Richie?"

Richie gave him a look of surprise before realisation dawned. "Oh shit…"

"Yeah. Ever since I was a kid."

"Fuck. I completely forgot, otherwise I'd never have asked for your help."

Jones laughed. "Yes, you would have, you selfish bastard."

"You've got me there. But seriously, you won't be in one of these for too long, and the Kingdom has more room than you're imagining."

"I fucking hope so, man. Otherwise, I'm not going to survive this one. At least the headlines will be funny. *Famous War Journalist Dies of Stress-Induced Heart Failure.*"

Richie let out a bark of laughter. "Uh-huh. I'll make sure young Priya writes them then. Okay, man, looks like Thompson is about to do his charm and schmarm thing. I've gotta get upstairs and get things ready." He held out his hand. "Good luck, man."

"Thanks. I think I'll need it."

11

"Jones, you've got to see this!" Priya exclaimed.

She was staring in awe out the small porthole. Beside her, Anna was doing the same. Jones, on the other hand, was desperately trying not to have a panic attack. He had already broken out in a cold sweat, and they had barely begun their journey to the hotel.

Outside the porthole, the water was becoming gradually darker the deeper they went. Fish and other types of marine life swam by, beautiful, somewhat startled by the weird metal creature that went past them. The old joke about a tin of people came to Priya's mind as she surveyed the alien world outside.

"Just try to breathe," Calder whispered to Jones. "Be over before you know it."

Somehow, Jones doubted that. But he appreciated the sentiment nonetheless. Anna and Priya were calling out the various things they saw. Priya commenting that she wished she could get photos.

"Oh we can get you some of those, ma'am," the pilot, an ex-marine named Jackson, said. "We had some professional photographers from the BBC come down to do it for us. I'll make sure to ask if we can give the ones we've not already used."

"Awesome!"

But the view soon turned into nothing but inky blackness. They had gone beyond the point that the light of the sun could reach. To a place where no natural light would ever reach. Jones found himself wondering what it would be like to live down there in the dark, dangerous depths.

He quickly dismissed the thoughts from his mind. There were some things that man was not meant to know, and the depths of the ocean were one of them. There was a reason it was one of the few truly unexplored places on earth, with 95% of it still being a complete mystery.

Yet here they were, heading down into the dark in a tiny submarine, to a giant underwater hotel called The Kingdom. Jones wondered if Thompson thought of himself as the god Poseidon. It would explain the name, and having met the man, he wouldn't have been surprised if that was the case.

There was something about his arrogance, to think that he could tame what billions of others had not, just because he had money. In the Greek myths, people that attempted to do what the gods had not meant them to had all suffered terrible fates for their hubris.

Jones caught himself staring out the porthole into the blackness, his gaze drawn to it. His thoughts were starting to blur, as if his mind were drifting through the dark water outside. But it was not drifting aimlessly—it was heading toward something.

Come to me…

Come to me…

Come to me…

"Jones!" Priya shouted, shaking him back to reality, a look of concern mixed with fear etched into her face.

"Sorry. I must have drifted off."

"You were talking," Anna said. There was a note of fear in her voice that sent a shiver down Jones' spine.

He saw that everyone's eyes were on him, even Jackson's, who had turned in his seat.

"What? What was I saying?"

"Come to me…"

***

As The Kingdom came into view through the small porthole, Thompson couldn't help but smile. He finally felt good. The overwhelming anxiety that had been plaguing him since the first moment he dreamt up the project had finally begun to lift, and now that he was on his way toward his dream, he could feel the tension easing.

The Kingdom was a circular, dome-like structure located in the middle of an expansive and flat part of the ocean floor. Lights dotted the exterior, with the central dome shining bright like a beacon. It was made out of specialised glass, strong enough to withstand the ocean's pressures, just so his guests could dine with a view of the ocean and its inhabitants overhead.

He had no idea how long it had taken him to get to this moment. Ever since he had first seen it in his dream, he had felt an overwhelming desire to achieve it—no matter what it cost. With drive, determination, investors, and billions of dollars, he had kept at it, until he had even fallen off the list of Forbes billionaires.

The years had blurred together into one great amalgam of business meetings, negotiations, and sleepless nights. It was as if something was behind him, spurring him on through the days when he felt like he had nothing left to give.

He'd lost his trophy wife, his kids, even his damn dog when the bitch had taken it from him.

"Your damn pet project means more to you than I do!" she'd screamed at him, tears and snot streaming down her once pretty face.

All he could think was—*how could I have loved something so ugly?*

Smudged running makeup, her surgically enhanced features contorted into a ghoulish mask of anger. There was something uncanny about her, as if she wasn't really human at all, more of a shell, a doll moulded to look human and somehow given the ability to speak.

Her anger didn't do much except annoy him, because any time spent dealing with her was less time spent achieving what he needed to. For a brief moment, he had considered hitting her. It would have shut her up, sent her scurrying away to her hole.

He'd been tempted. Oh, so tempted. One quick movement of the hand and she would have quieted, a look of shock spreading across her plastic face, almost human but not quite. Fortunately, he had stopped himself. Not because it was the right thing to do, not because of some misguided moral code, but because it would have delayed him further.

"Take what you want and get out. I've got work to do."

But none of that mattered anymore. Because here it was, in front of him. The thing he had worked so hard to make a reality. And it was beautiful. True beauty, not some plastic imitation of it. Designed by experts at the top of their game. A marvel of engineering.

He wasn't even sure how they'd done it. He had just done what he did best—find the right people for the job and get them to do their thing. And it was looking like it had paid off, if the gasps from the guests with him were anything to go by.

The smile that spread across Thompson's face was his first genuine one in ages. He just hoped that he could trust Calder and his team to handle whatever was happening in the medical bay.

12

Calder watched the last sub surface in front of him, popping out of the water in a spray of water. It only had a couple of his security team in it. The guests had already been led to the dining area by Thompson, where canapés and champagne awaited them, although some would have probably been wise to lay off the latter.

Priya, Anna, and Jones had all followed the guests. It seemed the young girl had taken a real liking to the journalists. Calder had also noticed a few sideways glances directed at the lovely photographer.

"Come in, boss," Ekkow came in through the comms. "Jackson and I are going to check out the med bay. Guests are squared away in the ballroom."

"Roger that."

The last of his crew climbed out of the sub, and Calder turned on his heel. He moved through the plush corridor, past the reception area, and down a grand, carpeted hallway toward the ballroom. Pushing his way through the double doors at the end brought a wave of laughter and chatter.

The ballroom was a majestic space. Grand marble floors, impressive pillars reaching up to a domed glass ceiling that gave a view of the waters outside. The glass was something Thompson's R&D team had cooked up, some revolutionary new substance that could hold back the pressures of the ocean.

At the other end of the room was a grand staircase that led up to an over-hanging balcony. Thompson was there, with a full band playing behind him. He was beaming, a microphone gripped tight in his hand. It was time for his speech.

As Thompson started to waffle, Calder noticed that Jones wasn't paying attention. His eyes were fixated on the ocean above, his face deathly pale.

"You okay, mate?"

The journalist didn't answer. He just kept staring. Calder followed his eyes, trying to see what he was looking at.

"There's something up there," Jones whispered. "I saw it, crawling across the glass."

After a few moments squinting at the ceiling, Calder spoke. "I don't see anything."

"It was there. I saw it move."

"Outside?"

Jones nodded. A chill ran down Calder's spine as he turned his eyes back to the dome above. He could barely hear Thompson droning on about vision and achievement. His hand drifted to the comforting heft of the pistol in its holster.

Reason was telling him that Jones was overreacting. That it had been some sort of fish or deep-sea creature. But reason couldn't explain the feeling that something was wrong down there. He'd felt it since stepping off the sub. There was something in the air, as if *wrong* had a taste and scent.

It was there on the tip of his tongue. Tingling in his nostrils. Calder had smelled something like it before. Back in Afghanistan, he'd found a hospital where they'd been implanting IEDs in kids. One of their "patients" had died on the table, a young boy of ten or eleven. They'd left him to rot, a gaping wound in his stomach, surgical equipment stained with dried blood haphazardly strewn around.

He'd been there a few days. There was the metallic smell of blood hanging in the air. The putrid stench of flesh rotting in the desert heat. Cloying, overwhelming. Two of his men had puked immediately. But Calder had just stared, horror and anger welling up inside him. He'd never be able to forget that sight, or that smell.

It was something like that was in the air now. Now that Jones had drawn his attention to it, he noticed that The Kingdom reeked of it. He looked around, trying to place it.

The crowd had taken on an unearthly, fake quality. It was as if the beautiful people around him were nothing more than plastic flesh stretch over robot skeletons. Thompson's voice seemed slurred and distorted, like he was speaking through a filter.

Calder fought the urge to draw his pistol. His hand was shaking. He gripped his weapon, wanting desperately to draw and fire on the crowd of people. They didn't seem like people, more like grotesque caricatures given life and voice by some unearthly force.

"Calder," came a voice, soft and smooth and full of care.

The ex-soldier blinked. Priya stood in front of his, her hands cupping his face.

"What happened?"

He looked around. Thompson had stopped speaking. The crowd was going about their party. Jones was seated in a chair, Anna gripping his hand tightly.

"You and Jones were acting odd. You were both pale, sweating. Can you take your hand off of your gun now, please?"

Slowly, he released his pistol. "We need to get out of here."

Just then, the lights went out.

***

"Come in, boss," Ekkow said into his mic. "Jackson and I are going to check out the med bay. Guests are squared away in the ballroom."

"I feel like I'm carrying too much firepower to check on a sick man," Jackson said, checking his shotgun.

"Thought you Marines loved your guns?"

"If you can believe it, I voted for gun control. I've seen too many accidental deaths in my time."

"Amen, bruv. But we follow orders, and the boss says bring the big guns to this thing."

"What does he expect us to find?"

"I don't know. Calder has a bad feeling. To tell you the truth, so do I."

"Fuck me, I'm glad I'm not the only one. Ever since we got down here, the air has been…"

"Wrong," Ekkow finished for him and shuddered. "This place ain't right, bruv."

The two men walked down plush corridors, past numbered rooms and windows that the dark expanse of the ocean floor. Soon the carpet under their feet turned to steel, their combat boots clanging on the hard surface as they walked. The exquisitely wallpapered walls gave way to brushed steel.

"Guess they have a very clear line between maintenance and guest areas," Jackson said.

"Yeah, man. You really think Thompson would waste the finer things on stuff the guests probably won't see?"

They continued down the grey, featureless corridors, past store rooms and staff quarters. In another five minutes, they were outside the med bay. The door was sealed, a sign above it flashing "Quarantine." A small comms unit was set into the side of the door. Ekkow keyed it.

"Doctor Goldstein? This is security, we've been sent to check on your situation. Do you have an update for us?"

"It's Goldstein here. We're still supposed to be under quarantine. We have a possible biological threat here."

"So how do we proceed?"

"Ideally, you get a hazmat team down here, and we go from there. I—"

The speakers cut out. Ekkow caught the tail end of mumbled conversation before the comm went down.

"Doc?"

In response, a scream came through. It crackled and buzzed, the sound too loud for the cheap, tinny speakers.

Ekkow looked to Jackson. The ex-marine's eyes darted briefly to the flashing quarantine sign above the door. Red light gave his expression an unearthly quality.

"Fuck it," he said. "Who really wants to live forever?"

13

Ekkow and Jackson took up positions either side of the door, their shotguns held ready. Both men nodded, before Ekkow pushed the button next to the door. The metal door slid open with a whooshing sound.

Ekkow went in weapon first, covering the left side. Jackson followed, covering right. The room was pitch black, the only light coming in from the hall. Glass crunched under their boots.

"Doc?" Ekkow called.

A piercing, inhuman shriek came from the darkness, the sound assaulting Ekkow's ears like sharp needles were being jammed into his eardrums. He swung his shotgun toward the sound, only to see the darkness coming at him.

Before he knew it, something had slammed into him. He flew backward, hitting the wall with a hard thump, his shotgun sailing off into the darkness. There was a thunderous boom and a blinding flash of light as Jackson fired, the shot aimed out the door.

Ekkow was struggling to breathe and get to his feet at the same time, but failing to do either. His legs were jelly, his vision blurred. Someone was screaming something about killing it. There was another shotgun blast as he struggled to get up. And suddenly, deafening silence.

"What the fuck was that?" Jackson breathed.

There was someone at Ekkow's side, holding him down, shining a pen light into his eye, checking his vitals. Dimly, he realised it had to be the doctor. He pushed the hands away from him and stood, drawing his pistol.

"Where did it go?" he asked, leaning heavily against the doorframe.

"Down there. Fuck it was fast. I couldn't get a bead. What the fuck was it?"

"It was Frank," Goldstein said. "He came out of the quarantine area and went crazy. Tried to kill… Oh God."

Goldstein raced back into the lab. He was calling a name, searching for the other man that had been in the room. Ekkow pulled a torch out of his pocket and clicked it on.

"This may help," he said, handing it to the doctor. "Jackson, I need you to get on comms. Get Calder on the line, report what just happened. He needs to get the guests out of here now. Doc, we need a description of Frank."

And that's when the lights went out.
***

Frank was running, his arms pumping, his strides long. If anybody had been timing, they'd have seen him breaking records as he sped through the corridors. But he wasn't the one in control.

The man was trying to scream. To shriek, or cry. To make any sound. But he couldn't. Whatever had control wouldn't let him. His skin felt wrong, like it wasn't his anymore. The pounding in his head was worse than any migraine he'd ever felt, as if his brain was banging itself against his skull over and over.

All he could feel was the pounding of his head. And heat. Intense, unbearable heat, like he was being cooked from the inside-out.

There was something inside his skull. It was moving through his mind, probing his memories. It was learning. A black, shapeless presence moved through the inner corridors of his subconscious, shifting through memories like a researcher going through textbooks.

Memories of his childhood in New York, of working with his father at the docks, of his mother's face, his ex-wife, his kids. It looked at them and tossed them aside, deciding for itself what was important and what wasn't. Family, friends, images, feelings, none of it mattered to this thing, so it deleted them.

Frank could feel himself getting erased. Slowly, deliberately, the thing was deleting him. He was terrified. A sheer, uncontrollable terror that surged through him. He tried to beg for mercy, or death, but the thing did not care.

As his mind slipped away, Frank came to the terrible realisation that whatever was inside him was more than he could ever know, and he was nothing. Just a tool to be used and discarded. A toy. And this thing had plans for everyone else in The Kingdom.

14

"Everybody remain calm!" Thompson shouted from the balcony. "It's a minor technical glitch! I'm sure my engineers are on it as I speak!"

The rich and very drunk were getting restless. They weren't accustomed to things going wrong, and they were not about to take this particular slight lightly. Some were muttering amongst themselves, others were talking to their security. The waiters and waitresses were doing their best to keep everyone in high spirits, and had even started rolling out the chairs and tables.

"Calder, come in," came Jackson's voice in Calder's ear.

"Go for Calder." He listened intently as Jackson relayed what had just happened, plus a brief description of Frank. "Roger that. I'll radio all units. We do this by the book. Sweep the facility, find the target, and neutralise the threat."

Calder keyed his comm unit and put the word out to all his men. People in the ballroom were getting restless, their chatter becoming louder. He could feel the tension in the room.

"Stay here," he said to Jones, Priya, and Anna, before jogging up the stairs to Thompson. "We have a situation."

Thompson listened to Calder's hurried description of events. "Fuck."

"I've instructed my men to seal off this area. Until we find Frank, no one leaves this room."

"Can't they go to their rooms?"

Calder shook his head. "They stay here, Thompson. No arguments. I'm in charge now, yeah?"

"What the hell is going on?" Jones asked, once Calder came downstairs again.

"It sounds like one of the employees went rogue. I'm waiting on a report from Ekkow and Jackson, but for now, I need you guys to stay here with the guests."

As he spoke, members of his security team were going to the exits. Each man closed a door and took up position beside it, with their hands on their weapons. Other members of staff were getting everyone a table and a seat. Red emergency lights gave the area a hellish glow.

Jones looked worried. "Any chance I can have a weapon?"

Calder eyed him. "You get the feeling you'll need it?"

"The way our day is going so far, I'd love a bazooka, but I'll settle for a handgun if I have to."

Calder chuckled. He signalled to one of his men.

"Can't give you a gun, but I'll give you the next best thing, mate. Eric," he said to his man, "you look after these three, yeah? They're more important than any of these other knobs in here, alright?"

***

"I need some help in here!" Goldstein called.

Ekkow went into the med bay to find it in ruins. Shelves were smashed, medical supplies were strewn about the floor, chairs had been tossed about. The doctor was kneeling in the corner of the room next to George. The man was propped up, his face a mask of intense pain. Sweat ran down his forehead.

"What do you need, doc?" Ekkow asked, rushing to his aid.

"Hold his leg still."

Ekkow did as he was told. Goldstein rushed off to the corner of the room and came back seconds later with a splint.

"Now you need to listen to me very carefully, big man—I'm going to need to splint his leg."

The big soldier had seen a lot in his time in the SAS, but the next few seconds still turned his stomach. As he held the splint, the doctor found where the man's leg had snapped. Without any preamble, he snapped the two halves of the bone back into place.

The man screamed in agony as Goldstein went to work splinting the leg. He was rough, but precise, and soon the job was done. The broken leg was splinted and wrapped tight. Goldstein stood and rushed off again.

"This will help with the pain, George," he said as he came back. He jabbed a needle into the man's arm. It didn't take long for the morphine to do its work.

"Jesus, bruv," Ekkow said. "That was rough."

Goldstein said nothing. He went over to a body that Ekkow hadn't noticed. After a quick check for a pulse, he sighed heavily.

"Frank do that?"

The doctor nodded. "We were talking to you, then Frank came back into the room. His eyes were like black pools. Sent chills down my spine. He just went crazy. Picked up my orderly and snapped his neck. George tried to get out the way, and Frank swatted him aside like he weighed nothing. Then you came in."

"You're telling me he's already killed someone?" Goldstein nodded. "Fuck. Jackson, you get that?"

"Yeah. Relaying it to the boss now."

"Where's Billy, doc?" Ekkow asked.

Goldstein stood and led the way to where Billy was. Ekkow peered through the small window into the room. He could just make out a man lying on a gurney in the dim light.

"Frank went in there, I'm guessing," the doctor remarked.

"What are we dealing with here?"

"Something biological. Although its structure is unlike anything else I've ever seen. I studied a sample under the microscope. My best guess is that this black goop got into Billy in the maintenance tunnels."

"Goop?"

"I know it sounds strange, but that's the best description I have. In fact, Frank…"

Goldstein noticed something. He studied the pants legs of one of the hazmat suits on the wall.

"Fuck. Frank's infected."

"How do you know?"

To answer the question, the doctor stuck his finger through the rip in the suit.

"This day just keeps getting better and better."

Just then, the body on the gurney moved, sitting upright. Ekkow heard the man inside groan.

"Billy!" Goldstein called.

The head turned in their direction. "Doc Goldstein?"

"Can you tell me how you feel?"

Billy clutched at his head. "Like I have the worst hangover in history. Where the fuck am I?"

"You're in the med bay. Do you remember how you got here?"

A shake of the head. "No. I remember being in the tunnels, hitting my head… Nothing else. Why the hell am I locked in here? Why is it dark?"

"Just relax. I'll explain everything to you soon. But for now, I just want you to lie down, okay?"

"Don't have to tell me twice, doc."

Goldstein started to slip into his hazmat suit. Ekkow placed an arm on his shoulder.

"I wouldn't do that, bruv."

"I have to," Goldstein said, shrugged off the man's hand. "You can cover me from out here. That man needs help. Now let me do my job. Maybe I can redeem myself somewhat."

Ekkow wondered about that last line, but decided it was best not to ask. "Okay. I'll cover you from here. But at the first sign of trouble, I want you out of there, yeah?"

"Oh don't you worry. I'll be out of there faster than a bullet."

15

The suit was hot and cloying. It was like Goldstein had just sealed himself in a sauna. A claustrophobic hotbox that cut off his peripheral vision. He smelt stale sweat from when he'd last worn the thing. He jumped as the door behind him sealed shut.

"Billy, I want you to stay on right there, alright?" Goldstein said.

His heart was thudding hard in his chest. Frank had picked up George like he was nothing, snapped John's neck like a twig. Whatever this was, it made people dangerous. And here he was trapped in a small room with what amounted to Patient Zero.

Billy did as he was told, lying flat on the table. His eyes, wide and full of fear, were glued to the doctor, following him everywhere.

"You're scaring me, doc."

"It's going to be alright, young man. Just let me examine you."

Goldstein set his bag down carefully next to Billy and went about a physical examination, using his small penlight as he did so. He struggled not to jump every time Billy moved.

What struck him was that Billy was in great shape. The wound on his head was gone, there were no outward signs of any injuries, and his pupils reacted well. Apart from a light fever, the man was in the peak of health. A far cry from how he had been when they had first brought him into the med bay.

"How do you feel?"

"Um… My mouth feels like it's stuffed with cotton wool, my head is pounding, and I'm really queasy, but otherwise I feel fine, doc."

"Okay. I'm just going to draw some blood."

He half expected the blood to come out pitch black, but no. It looked normal. Goldstein was as relieved as he was puzzled.

"Okay, young man, I want you to take two of these, and drink as much water as you can manage. You seem pretty dehydrated, but other than that, all good."

"So I can come out?"

"Not yet. Let me run a couple more tests."

"What's your professional opinion?" Ekkow asked as the doctor clumsily got out of the suit.

"He looks healthy. I need to check the blood, but I must admit something."

"What?"

"I am way out of my depth. No pun intended."

***

"Calder, this is Smith, come in."

"Roger that, Smith, what you got?"

"We're in one of the corridors leading up to maintenance. We've got what looks like blood on the floor, ripped pieces of clothing, and…" There was a pause. "Jesus Christ."

"What is it?"

"Pieces of flesh, boss. At least, that's what we think it is."

"Think?"

"Yeah. It's like rubber almost. No blood, nothing. Wait, think I see something… Hands up where I can see them!"

"Smith, what do you see?"

"Not sure. Too dark to… Fuck! Contact!"

The comms went dead. Calder spent a minute trying to get them back, but it was no use. He radioed their last position and sent two teams as backup.

"What the fuck did we just walk into?"

He looked up, took in the number of people, and did a quick calculation in his head. He had to get them out. Taking the stairs two at a time, he ran to the balcony. Thompson gave him a surprised look as he stood at the railing.

"Ladies and gentlemen!" Calder yelled. Gradually, the conversation died down. "I need your attention, please! I want everyone to get in groups of three and form a line. We're going to be heading back to the subs so that we can get to the surface."

"Axel, what the fuck do you think you're doing?" Thompson snarled.

Calder turned and was about to rip into the man when he heard the shots. His radio crackled to life.

"Boss, we've got contact. Smith is down, I repeat, Smith—" the signal cut off.

Booming shotgun blasts could be heard echoing down the corridors. The staccato sound of a pistol being fired. Panic started to spread through the crowd.

"Security teams! Get them ready to move!" Calder called, unhooking the latch on his holstered Sig.

"What's happening?" Anna asked.

"Gunfire," Jones said. "Something bad is going down. Anna, Priya, I want you two to stay close."

Eric unshouldered his shotgun and nodded reassuringly to the group. Calder was coming down the stairs, Thompson hot on his heels.

"Eric," Calder said, "get these three to the subs. Now."

"Axel!" Thompson said. "Listen to me, you fucker. I pay your fucking salary!"

Calder whirled around and grabbed the man by his lapels. "Listen to me, fucker! I'm getting these people out of here *now*. You can stay if you want, but if not, follow Eric and get to the fucking surface!"

Thompson's face was a mask of surprise. He couldn't reply, just opened and closed his mouth silently, like a fish out of water. The look in Calder's eyes had robbed him of his anger.

"Ekkow, come in."

"Yes, boss?"

"We're evacuating. I'm going to head to the control room first. I need to get the power on. Send Jackson to rendezvous with me. I want you to get the doc and the other two to safety."

"Boss, there's a slight issue. Billy is still under quarantine."

"Fuck." He didn't want to bring whatever this was back to the surface. Neither did he want to leave Billy down there with the hostile around.

"Boss?"

"I'm thinking."

A moment of silence passed before Ekkow spoke. "Get them to the surface, Axel. I'll stay with Billy. This is a good defensible position. Jackson can get the doc and George to the subs."

"Roger that. Keep yourself safe, mate."

"Always, bruv."

Calder looked around again. Half his team were efficiently organising the crowd into groups while the other half watched the doors. He tried hailing the men who'd called contact, but was getting nothing. There was a good chance they were dead. He had no idea how one man could take out six trained soldiers, but it wasn't the time to speculate. It was time to compartmentalise and get shit done.

Pushing his way through the crowd, Calder found what he was looking for on the opposite wall. He'd insisted Thompson install and emergency warning system in case anything went wrong. Hidden in an innocuous wall panel was a big red button. He smacked his palm against it.

An alarm started to sound. It was the signal for everyone inside The Kingdom to get to the submarine bay as fast as they could.

"This is Calder," he said into his throat mike. "I'm heading to the control room. I'll relay a sitrep ASAP. I want a team to keep an eye on the section where the last team was sighted. Do not engage until I have further information. I repeat, do not engage."

The control room was at the heart of The Kingdom. Almost everything could be managed from there. But Calder needed access to the CCTV. He and his men were blind, and he needed eyes on the threat.

There wasn't much time as his team were already starting to lead the guests out the ballroom. He took off at a run.

16

The panic really set in once the alarm started to sound. Some people kept their heads, some started yelling. Intermittent screams broke out. Priya did what she could to document it all. Snapping pictures of the panicking crowd, painted a ghostly red by the emergency lighting, of Thompson's desperate attempts to calm everyone, and of the clinical efficiency of Calder's security team as they started the evacuation.

"Miss, I'm going to need you to stick close," Eric said, grabbing Priya's arm.

She resisted the urge to fight her way out of his grip. He was doing his job and didn't need someone to lose their head. She could feel her anxiety rising, like a tide within her chest.

Taking a step back, she continued to take pictures. The security teams had started to lead people out the doors toward the submarine bay. Priya could hear chatter coming through Eric's radio as the teams communicated with each other. It looked like Calder had trained them well.

"Okay, guys, Mr. Thompson, I'm going to need you all to follow me. We have a sub ready and waiting for us. We just have to get there."

Thompson looked defeated, like all the air had been let out of him. His shoulders slumped, his white teeth hidden behind slack lips. He'd stopped shouting. Even his suit looked the worse for wear in the ghastly red light. He just nodded and fell in line behind Jones.

Priya felt sorry for Calder's men. They were struggling to hold people from surging through the doors toward the subs. A couple of the crowd were having to be helped forward they were so drunk. The noise was deafening. Priya was starting to sweat, the temperature of the room rising as the crowd got more agitated.

"It's like a slaughterhouse," she heard Eric mutter.

She saw what he meant. If whatever was out there decided to attack them now, a lot of people were going to die.

Soon it was their turn to move and Eric was hustling them forward. Each team was in constant contact with the others. A constant stream of reports was being filtered in. Eric responded every now and then, calling in their position as they moved.

Priya tried to focus on her job, on the pictures, but she could feel the panic rising. Her hands were starting to shake.

Not now, please not now.

She tried to slow her breathing. In through her nose, and out through her mouth. Slow and steady. Slow and steady. But it was coming, she could feel it. Rising like bile in her throat, threatening to take over. She put her hand on the wall to steady herself.

"You okay?" Jones asked, holding her to steady her.

She shook her head, continuing to focus on her breathing. Jones had to hold her up.

"Eric, hold up!"

The security man stopped. "She okay?"

Priya tried to wave them off, to breathe normally, but her chest was constricted. Her breathing was coming in short, sharp gasps.

"Come on, Priya, it's okay. You're alright."

Jones' tone was soothing, his words cutting through the chaos and noise around them.

"Fuck. This," Priya said.

She sank to the floor and closed her eyes. Shifted her focus to her breathing. In through her mouth, feeling the air slowly fill her lungs and belly, then leave as she exhaled. She pictured her happy place. Her room as a child, sat at her desk, tapping away on the old typewriter that had once belonged to her grandmother.

"This too shall pass," she said, repeating it over and over, the very same words her grandmother had said to her every time she'd had an attack as a child.

Eric looked over his shoulder. They were almost the last in line. Another security man was waving them over. He shook his head. He had to wait; if the journalist had a full-blown panic attack, there was a good chance she'd get seriously injured.

It took a minute, but finally Priya opened her eyes again. Jones offered his hand.

"Good to have you back," he said, hoisting her up.

"Let's get the fuck out of here," she said, slinging her camera over her shoulder.

Eric nodded and set off after the retreating group. Jones gave Priya a smile, following Eric, Anna by his side. Thompson brought up the rear, seemingly in his own world.

"Everyone hold. I see something up ahead," came a voice through Eric's comms.

Eric held up his hand in a fist, and the group stopped. Priya could just hear the security teams trying to shush the crowd. The silence fell down the corridor like a wave, coming from the front and moving backward.

"I'm going to check it out," came the voice from the radio.

The silence was somehow worse than the chatter. Priya struggled to keep her breathing steady. Sweat rolled down her forehead.

"Contact!"

Gunshots boomed down the corridor. Shotguns and small arms fire going off simultaneously. The crowd panicked. The ones at the front struggled to flee, stopped by those behind them. It wasn't long before Priya's group saw a stampede of panicked people heading straight for them.

"Fuck me," she said as she turned to run.

***

"Contact!"

Ekkow heard the call come over the radio and gripped his shotgun. Jackson had already taken the others off, leaving Ekkow to barricade himself in the med bay. The waiting was the worst part, and now, instead of engaging the enemy, he had to stay put.

"What's going on?" Billy asked, face pressed up against the glass.

"Security has it in hand, bruv."

He lowered the volume on his radio. The reports were scattered and disjointed, making his comrades sound more like panicked amateurs than the trained soldiers that they all were. Whatever was out there, it was scary enough to override years of training and combat experience. He could hear the fear in their voices, the utter senseless terror.

Ekkow wanted to be out there with them, facing the enemy head-on. If he could see it, know what it was, then he wouldn't have been as scared as he was. Fear of the unknown is the worst thing, ever. Always had been.

The man was almost tempted. All he had to do was lock the door behind him and get into the fight. It wouldn't take long to get there. But he had his orders. He wasn't going to disobey them without a very good reason to do so.

"Help me!" Billy screamed.

Ekkow spun around. Billy had his back pressed up tight against the door, his fists banging on it. And what could be seen just over his shoulder made Ekkow's blood run cold.

17

Jackson, Goldstein, and George were making their way to the submarine bay when the screaming started. Jackson was on point, Goldstein supporting George as they walked behind him. The screams and gunshots stopped all three dead in their tracks.

"Doc, I want you to stay here with George. If anything starts coming, I'll hold them off and you get back to Ekkow. Understood?"

Goldstein nodded. He couldn't speak, his mouth dry, his throat constricted with fear. It wasn't the gunshots. It was the inhuman screams, some of which were being cut short.

"Fuck this job," George said through clenched teeth. "I could have been sitting in a cosy office, but no, Jackie said I needed the fucking money…"

Jackson ignored George's muttered complaints and started forward. The chatter coming through the radio was useless. Panicked reports of contact with an unknown enemy and men being taken down. This could only mean one thing—whatever was attacking them had efficiently dismantled Calder's specially selected team of operators.

The ex-marine shook his head to clear it. Now wasn't the time for speculation. He had to deal with what was in front of him. What was happening elsewhere didn't matter.

Blocking out the screams, gunfire, and panicked radio chatter, he moved forward. He made no sound, taking each step carefully. Wherever his eyes went, so did the barrel of his shotgun. The corridor took a meandering left turn up ahead, which would lead to the path to the submarine bay—and whatever was attacking his comrades.

Breathing steady, heartrate somehow calmed, Jackson advanced. He was almost at the turn when a shadow moved. Something was heading toward him. He stopped, shotgun ready.

There was a sound, like claws skittering on steel. It was getting closer. Jackson didn't have time to signal to Goldstein, so he kept his attention focused.

Whatever was making the inhuman skittering was almost in sight. A weird shadow was cast on the wall, just visible in Jackson's peripheral vision. He couldn't focus on it, but had a vague impression of elongated limbs and a skinny form. He figured he maybe had a few seconds before it came into view.

As the creature came around the corner, Jackson's training took over. He was opening fire before he could comprehend was he was seeing. The monstrosity jerked as the rounds tore into it, spraying black, gelatinous fluids onto the walls.

Jackson pumped the shotgun and fired again. He'd shut down his mind, unable to deal with what he was seeing in front of him. He had one job—protect the civilians.

"Get to Ekkow!" Jackson heard himself screaming, firing again as another creature came into view.

Goldstein's response was drowned out by another shotgun blast—Jackson's last shell. He didn't have time to reload, so he dropped the long weapon, drawing his pistol from his holster and opening fire in one smooth motion.

More things were coming round the corner and Jackson kept firing, his rounds tearing globules of flesh out of his targets. He heard the dry click of an empty magazine, ejected it, and slid in a fresh one before the empty had even hit the floor.

As he fired, he moved back, retreating down the corridor, knowing he didn't have many magazines left. For a brief second, he considered calling for backup, but if these things were here, then there was no backup to call for.

They were getting closer, climbing over their wounded, their movements unlike any living creature Jackson had ever seen. Somewhere in the back of his mind, the ex-marine knew he was going to die.

He had survived three tours, six IEDs, one ambush, and even three rounds to the chest. But he was done now. He was going to die down here, in the cold darkness at the bottom of the ocean, and there was nothing he could do about it.

His slid his last magazine into his weapon, the clatter of the empty one as it hit the floor drowned out by the deafening roar of small arms fire in the tight corridor.

"Oorah, motherfuckers!"

***

The ops room was a mess. Upturned chairs, shattered glass, and torn paper were scattered all over the floor. There was blood on the walls and ceiling, like some twisted modern art painting, but no bodies.

"Fucking hell," Calder said, lowering his Sig.

The enemy had probably hit the ops room first, taking out the lights in The Kingdom. And then, what? Headed to the submarine bay to let in reinforcements?

What the fuck are we fighting?

Calder grabbed a chair and sat in front of the bank of monitors. Most were smashed to shit, but a couple were still working. Grabbing a keyboard and mouse, Calder started tapping keys.

He was trying to bring up the cameras nearest the battle, but was getting nothing, meaning they weren't working. He swore and instead called up the next closest ones. The first picture he got was of Priya, Anna, Thompson, Jones, and Eric. The security man was shouting something and directing fire down the corridor.

There was nothing Calder could do for them, so he moved on. He didn't find Jackson and his group on any of the cameras. On a couple, he caught a glimpse of something shooting past, but it was too quick to get a clear picture of what it was.

He switched to the medical bay feed. The first image was that of Billy, pressed up against the door, a look of pure terror in his face. Another camera switch, trying to get a view of what he was seeing. But all Calder got was an image of Ekkow's back. His friend was readying his shotgun, getting ready to enter the quarantine room.

Calder tried his radio, trying to get Ekkow to respond, but the man didn't seem to even register the call. Calder swore again. A quick glance at the map on the wall showed him what he already knew. That the shortest way to his friend was through the chaos, and he couldn't risk it.

The Kingdom was basically a big central area, where all the shops, ballroom, casino, restaurants, and bars were, with the rest of it laid out in a circular pattern that surrounded the middle. Corridors led off from the centre area to the staff quarters, guest rooms, maintenance places, submarine bay, and medical bay. There were also several side sections dedicated to power, oxygen, and other essential things that kept the facility running.

Calder considered his options. Ekkow was in trouble and he had a choice. If he stayed in the control room, he could try and direct escape efforts—although with most of the cameras out of commission, including those in the submarine bay, this wouldn't be of much help. Plus, he'd be leaving Ekkow to fend for himself against an unknown threat.

The fastest way to get to his friend was to cut through the middle of the facility, then veer off at a right angle toward the med bay. If he legged it, he would take about ten minutes. Assuming he didn't encounter hostiles.

"Buggeration," Calder said.

He let his instincts take over. Ekkow had saved his life in Afghan. Dragged him from his vehicle after the IED hit, while under heavy enemy fire.

Time to repay the favour.

Calder took off running.

***

Goldstein was struggling to carry George as fast as he could manage. He could hear the screams behind him. The man was heavier than he looked, and his arms were aching. They just needed to get a little way down the corridor. He wasn't going to leave him behind.

Which was why he was so confused where the man *disappeared.*

Goldstein skidded to a stop. What the hell had just happened? He was there one moment and gone the next.

He looked around the corridor, and then he noticed the open door. Moving cautiously, he advanced toward it. Inside was nothing but darkness.

"George?" he asked.

A whimper came from out of the pitch-black room in reply. Then something shot out of the darkness and wrapped itself around Goldstein's foot. He let out a cry of surprise as it pulled him off his feet.

He hit the ground hard, his head bouncing off the floor. Dazed and confused, he only barely aware that he was being dragged into the darkened room toward an unknown fate.

18

Gunfire. Inhuman screams of terror. People scrambling past, climbing over each other to save themselves. It was like being back in a war zone. And on some strange level, it was making Jones feel alive.

The five of them were trying to back away from whatever was coming, but the stampede of panicked people was making it difficult. Eric had tried shouting for calm, but whatever these people had seen made them blind with fear. Every now and then, they heard the boom of a shotgun or the shots from a pistol, but even that was almost overwhelmed by the screams.

The corridor smelled of blood, sweat, fear, and cordite. The group fought their way through the stream of people, Jones using his stocky build as a battering ram to clear a path, Anna's hand clenched tightly in his own. In the middle, Thompson gibbered incoherently as they moved. Priya was right behind him, with Eric bringing up the rear.

"I need a sitrep."

Eric had been trying to get a hold of his men for ages, but all he was getting was confused, incoherent reports. Jones didn't hold out much hope on the security men stopping the threat. He knew it wasn't human.

There was a feeling in his bones. A feeling that something dark and sinister was coming to slaughter them. He could feel its perverse glee as it killed the people behind him, could sense the joy it was having. He didn't know how or why, but the thing was there, in his head, and it was grinning. They had to get away.

Ahead of them was a door that led off to the left, and Jones slammed himself against it as they passed, dragging Anna in with him. The others followed, Eric slamming the door shut behind them.

"What the fuck is going on?" Anna asked, panting.

"Something is coming," Jones said.

He looked around. They were in some sort of service tunnel that continued on for about five meters before ending in a T-junction. Pipes lined the walls.

"What about those people? Surely we can try and save them?" Priya asked.

"We need to look after ourselves," Jones said. "Forget those outside. They're panicked, scared, and have to look after their own. The only people that matter right now are the ones in front of you."

"We can't just—"

"Jones is right," Eric cut in. "I know it seems harsh, but we need to focus on ourselves."

"Where are we?" Jones asked, trying to change the subject.

"Service tunnel. If we go left, it leads to medical, and right ultimately ends at the rooms."

"Ekkow is there, isn't he?"

Eric nodded. "Jackson perhaps. I'd say it's our best choice. More guns won't be a bad thing."

"What about Calder?" Priya asked.

"He said he'd go to operations," Eric said, "so that he could get an idea of what was happening. I've had no contact since."

"Where's ops?" Jones said.

Eric pointed over his shoulder. "Back there."

"Medical it is then."

Jones went first, Anna gripping his hand tightly. Every now and then she flinched as a scream of terror, pain, or both came from behind the door. He did his best to block it out, like he used to do when he was in a combat zone.

Jones turned the corner, Anna and Priya followed, and Thompson went left. He walked slowly, seemingly unaware of what he was doing.

"Mr. Thompson!" Eric said, starting after him.

Priya grabbed Eric's arm, told him to stop, and jogged after the billionaire. She took him gently by the arm.

"Not this way. Come on. Take my hand."

There was a deafening wrenching sound and something hit the end wall of corridor with an almighty crash. Priya spun around, realising that it was the twisted remains of the door they had just come through.

She stared at the wreckage, trying to figure out what was wrong with it. Then it hit her, and she felt bile rising in her throat. Eric had been caught by the door as it was blown toward the wall. His left arm had been crushed against the wall and half his head was missing. His right eye remained open, staring unblinking down the hallway. Blood was everywhere.

Movement attracted her attention, and she saw Jones backing up, dragging Anna away and desperately motioning for her and Thompson to do the same.

There was a dreadful ticking sound coming toward them. It sounded like claws on metal, the *tic tic tic* of a dog's paws on a solid surface. But Priya knew that it was no dog.

She grabbed Thompson's hand and started backing up as fast as she dared. The man didn't resist, instead just following meekly. The ticking was getting closer.

Tic tic tic.

It sent chills down Priya's spine. She felt the goose pimples on her back, her hairs standing on end, every single fibre of her lizard brain screaming that there was danger nearby.

Jones had reached the door at his end. He opened it slowly, scared that it would make any kind of sound, and shoved Anna through. With one last glance behind him to make sure Priya was doing the same, he went through and shut the door behind him.

Just as Priya was closing her door, she saw a part of the creature come into view. A set of claws came around the corner, slick with blood and fluids, glimmering slightly in the stark lighting. The creature seemed to notice Eric's dead body, and there was this dreadful, inhuman hissing sound, which was the last thing she heard before she closed the door on the horrific scene.

19

Something was crawling into the medical bay, slithering its way through the vent into the room. Ekkow couldn't describe what it was, his brain just refused to make sense of it. Black, glistening, and *wrong*, it forced the mind to rebel, to reject what it was seeing.

The thing made the big man freeze in his tracks, his mind recoiling in horror. Billy was screaming hysterically, pounding on the doors with his fists, tears streaming down his face. The thing reminded him of the horror stories his gran had told him as a boy, about the things that dwelled in the dark and preyed on naughty children.

"Help me!"

Billy's frantic cries finally spurred him into action. He readied his weapon and slammed the button that disengaged the locks on the door. It slid open with a whoosh. Billy fell through, and Ekkow fired.

The pellets hit the creature, little dimples forming in the gooey black substance, but it made no sign of pain or distress. It just kept oozing into the room. Ekkow slammed the button again, sealing the thing in the room.

"What the fucking hell?"

"That's what attacked me in the tunnels!" Billy yelled, scrambling to his feet. "That fucking thing made me eat it, then forced its way out of me and into Frank."

"It *made* you eat it?"

"Yes! Now let's get the fuck out of here!"

The thing was still oozing slowly, heading for the door. Ekkow watched it carefully as he backed up. But something else was bugging him.

"You hear that?" he asked.

"Hear what?"

"Exactly. No gunfire. The fight is over, and I think we lost."

***

The silence was almost deafening. Calder stopped in his tracks, his mouth held open to cut out internal sound, and listened. Briefly, he considered the radio, but that wasn't a good idea. If anyone wanted to maintain radio silence to stay hidden, he'd be giving away their position.

He considered his options. The first was to head back to the ops room. He dismissed that immediately. Chances were that Ekkow still needed help.

Sticking with my second option then.

He moved fast but silently, rolling his feet to prevent his boots from clanging on the cold steel floor. So far, he hadn't come across anyone else. The corridors were empty and undisturbed. The eerie silence gave his surroundings a surreal quality.

Calder blinked. Something was wrong, but he couldn't place it. He stopped, listened, scanned for movement. The hallway was clear, and yet...

He took a deep breath, blinked again. Observed what was in front of him, weapon forward. Then he saw it. It was the walls. They were glistening.

He recoiled away from the wall closest to him, putting himself in the middle of the corridor. Something was oozing down the left and right walls. It glistened in the dim light, rippling and moving perversely. There was something else—a voice.

It wasn't distinct. More like a murmur, one that was trying to worm its way inside his ears, almost as if it was fighting to be heard. Calder couldn't describe the sound. It was like a buzzing, whispering, unnatural voice that came from everywhere and nowhere. The sound wasn't even physical. He wasn't hearing it as much as becoming aware of it. Or it was becoming aware of *him*.

Calder knew that the stuff on the walls was alive. And it was talking. For a moment, he couldn't move, trapped by some unnatural force. It *wanted* him, he could feel it. The whispering was becoming more distinct, going from jumbled garbling to letters.

The ex-SAS man shook his head. He needed to run, and he needed to do it now. Each step was a mission. His felt as if they were held down by weights, the soles of his boots glued to the floor for good measure. Out of desperation, he fired at the walls, the rounds being slurped up by the sticky black substance.

And then it screamed. A piercing, inhuman shriek that burst into Calder's mind like a pane of glass had just exploded inside his skull. The pain was almost unbearable, but he noticed that he could move again. He stumbled forward, putting more rounds into the walls, not caring where they went as long as they hit the substance.

The screaming continued, but became less and less prevalent in Calder's head. He started to regain his senses, breaking out into a jog, and then a full-on sprint. The thing was still trying to get into his head, unintelligible whispers still worming their way around his mind.

Suddenly, it was gone, but Calder kept running until he reached the med bay and collapsed into the room. Ekkow was by his side in his a moment, concern etched in his face. Billy was still staring at the creature in the other room.

"What happened?"

"Something… On the walls," Calder panted.

"Easy, easy," Ekkow said, moving his hand over Calder's pistol.

He realised he was still pulling the trigger, the firing pin clicking on the dry chamber over and over in a staccato rhythm. He stopped, ejected the spent magazine, and slowly slid in a fresh one before standing.

"We're not fighting a human enemy," Calder said.

"I know. Come and look at this."

Ekkow led him to the quarantine room. Calder peered through the window at the substance, which was still inching closer and closer to the sealed door.

"We have to move."

"Fucking A, man," Billy said, already heading for the door.

Ekkow stopped him. "Stay between us, mate. You can't go walking into these things headfirst."

"Calder, Ekkow, anyone, come in," came a voice over the comms. "We need someone with a very big gun right fucking now."

20

Jones stood with his ear against the door, listening. He wanted to know if Priya had gotten out alright. Instead, all he could hear was a sickening squelching sound that he dared not think about.

He gripped the pistol in his hand tighter. It had skittered across the floor toward him after the door had killed Eric. The weight of it gave him some comfort, although he doubted it would be much use judging by how much firepower had already been thrown at their enemy.

"Did she make it?" Anna whispered.

"I think so. Come on, we've got to move."

"But where?"

Jones didn't speak. He was thinking. Priya would need help, but he wasn't equipped for rescue at the moment. So he and Anna had to get to Calder or Ekkow. But where were they?

"We need to get a radio."

"Where?"

Jones looked back at the closed door. Anna shook her head.

"You're crazy."

"Look, we need to get in touch with the soldiers. And apart from the submarine bay, which might be swarming with whatever that is in there, Eric's radio is the only one within reach."

"Fuck. Do you have a plan?"

"Yeah. Don't get killed."

He smiled at her, raised his finger to his lips, and put his ear against the door again. The sounds had stopped. He listened for a bit longer.

"Anna, if something happens, I want you to run, you understand? Get to the medical bay and find Calder or Ekkow."

The young woman nodded. Jones gave her a half-hearted smile. He took a deep breath and slowly pushed the door open, listening for any sign of the movement on the other side. Hearing nothing, he went through before he had a chance to second-guess his decision. Like his father had said, never give yourself the time to talk yourself out of what needs doing.

Wishing that this hadn't been the first time in years that he'd held a weapon, he swept the corridor beyond. It was empty, except for the mangled door, and an unrecognisable mess of blood and cartilage on the floor that Jones could only assume was what was left of Eric's body.

Jones resisted the almost overwhelming urge to sprint down the corridor at top speed. He knew it would likely be suicide, so he forced himself to listen to his instincts. Trying to stick as close to what the soldiers he'd worked with had taught him, he stalked toward Eric's mutilated remains, his weapon going where his eyes went.

His heart was threatening to burst its way out of his chest as he moved. Everything seemed fine, but Jones couldn't shake the feeling he was being watched. The impulse to turn around nagged at him, making the little hairs on the back of his neck stand on end. He fought it, focusing on keeping the pistol he had trained in front of him.

It was about twenty feet to the body, and the journalist was counting every single one. Sweat beaded on his forehead, the cold confines of the undersea structure suddenly feeling as hot as the dusty towns of Afghanistan and Iraq.

Eighteen...

Nineteen...

He stopped, took a breath, and slowly peeked around the corner. The doorway they had all come through was reduced to nothing more than a ragged hole. The steel frame was bent and twisted, reflecting the force with which the door had been wrenched away from it.

The strength it would take... The thought flashed through Jones' mind.

He could see the plush carpet of the hall beyond, which had looked so grand and inviting when he had first walked it, but was now stained with blood and gore. Most importantly, however, the hallway was clear.

Turning back to the body, Jones almost gagged. Eric had been reduced to a bloody stain on the floor. The formerly heavily muscled special operator looked as if he'd been put through a wood chipper. There wasn't anything in the pile of gristle, blood, and cartilage that could be identified as human anymore.

Hoping that the radio hadn't been destroyed as well, Jones crouched down. With horrified fascination, he realised that the creature that had done this had cut through Eric's clothes very precisely, almost like a surgeon would in the ER. It was as if it had realised that the clothes were not part of the man himself.

This meant that there was more of a chance of the radio being intact, but it also meant that if it was, it was beneath the mess of gore. The sheer savageness of the butchery that had been done to the man was still working hard to make Jones lose his lunch, and the smell was much worse.

The coppery smell of blood was mingled with the incredible stench of bile and whatever else had been contained within the stomach and intestines. The overpowering miasma of foul smells was forcing Jones to breathe through his mouth. His lips were parted only slightly, as if he feared he'd inhale any of the former security man's body.

Keeping his weapon in his dominant hand, Jones plunged his other into the mess of nastiness in front of him. There was a revolting squelching sound as he searched for the man's body armour, making him gag. The sting of bile stayed at the bag of his throat, threatening to come up all over the dead man's remains.

Finding the edge of the almost surgically bisected clothes, Jones gripped it and flipped them over. The sickly wet slapping of soggy skin hitting the floor and the slopping of blood and whatever the fuck else was too much.

Jones turned his head quickly and violently threw up. Bile spewed out onto the steel floor, mixing with the blood and forming a yellowish, red goo that slowly made its way across the smooth steel underneath it.

He coughed and wretched a few times before throwing up again. This time, only a dribble of bile escaped his lips. Jones struggled to get his stomach under control, willing his body to stop. After a few shallow breaths, he turned back toward the mess. He was acutely aware of the feel of the gore on his hand as he did so.

If Eric hadn't have been wearing black clothes, Jones would not have been able to tell them apart from everything else by sight. He found the man's jacket and started to scrabble for the radio device.

Jones knew one of the creatures was coming. He could sense its presence.

His neck prickled. It was like a small charge of electricity had just hit him, running down his spine. A headache started to form. Starting small and slowly building in intensity, it was as if someone was driving a very small needle into his brain.

Tic...

Tic...

Tic...

The sound of claws on steel. He hurried to work his way through the mess, his fingers scrabbling desperately for the radio. His other hand gripped the pistol so tightly that they turned white.

Where the fuck is... THERE!

His hand brushed against a hard plastic rectangle. He grabbed it, spinning around as he did so, raising his weapon, finger on the trigger and about to tighten.

That's when it hit him. It was like a bodybuilder had just hit him with a perfect swing from a baseball bat. He felt his ribs crack as the breath was forced out of him and he was lifted off the floor. As he flew down the corridor, the gun went clattering away, spinning as it went, but he held onto the radio.

Jones hit the wall with a violent thump, his head banging into it. Stars formed in front of his eyes. His limbs refused to obey his commands, instead splaying out like those of a newborn giraffe. He fought for breath, his side sending waves of complete agony through his body. All he needed to do was reach the weapon.

The creature hissed, a wet, sticky, unnatural sound, like it was gurgling some viscous liquid. Its claws *tic tic tic'd* their way toward him, moving slowly, taking its time.

Jones fought to crawl away, but the floor offered no purchase for his scrabbling fingers. His heart thumped in his chest, the constant thudding combined with the roaring of his blood almost drowning out all external sounds.

He wanted to call out, to tell Anna to run, to do *something* other than just lay there waiting to die, but he couldn't. His body wouldn't cooperate, it wouldn't listen to the commands from his brain. All he could do was grip the radio, almost as if he wanted to die having accomplished one last good thing.

Thoughts of his brother flashed into his head. Was this how he had felt when he was dying? Had he thought of his sibling as well as he died in the sand, his lifeblood staining it red?

His thoughts were abruptly interrupted by gunshots, the explosions of cordite unbearably loud in the cramped steel corridor. At the same time, someone was screaming, a primal war cry of terror, fear, and anger. It was soon joined by another scream, but this one was wet, unearthly, and one of pain and surprise.

Jones became dimly aware of his arm being pulled. The gunfire continued as he was dragged along the corridor. A woman was shouting at him, the words indistinguishable, but the meaning clear.

Move!

He forced his legs to move, using every ounce of his strength to get them underneath himself. The gunfire had stopped, replaced by the dry click of an empty chamber. Jones gave one last push, getting himself up with the help of the person who had his arm.

The scream continued behind him, driving him forward. He stumbled on, being dragged along, and suddenly he was through the door. It was slammed shut behind him and they continued on, Anna desperately trying to get them to move faster, fear giving her a strength she had never experienced before.

Pain stabbed into Jones' side with each step, threatening to force the breath from his lungs, but he kept going. To stop would mean death. He did not want to die. Not now. Not miles beneath the ocean, torn up and turned into pulp like a frog in a blender.

There came an almighty crash from behind them, and Anna tried to move faster, gripping Jones' wrist tightly and dragging him along. The crash was followed by a scream that echoed down toward them, its meaning unmistakable.

The creature was hungry.

It was pissed off.

And it had its prey in its sights.

21

The gunfire made Priya stop. She tried to pinpoint their source, but The Kingdom was just a maze of corridors that made it next to impossible. Beside her, Thompson continued to talk to himself. The words were unintelligible, a bunch of gibberish that it seemed only he could understand.

It was surprising how small the big man looked. His white suit was stained with sweat, his hair askew. The polished veneer had fallen away, revealing a broken man underneath.

Although it would have been easier, and probably safer for her, to leave the man somewhere, Priya couldn't bring herself to do it. He was a person, and she had always believed that people deserved to be treated with kindness.

The gunshots faded, leaving her and Thompson standing alone in a quiet corridor. She had no idea where she was, and the myriad signs on the ceilings and walls didn't seem to be pointing her in the right directions. Some halls were even missing signs entirely.

Not for the first time she wondered just how close to completion the hotel actually was. It seemed that in his haste to get more investors, Thompson had cut several corners. Had he compromised on safety as well?

She shook the thoughts out of her head. Right now, she had one job—link up with Calder and Ekkow. Whatever was roaming the halls was a serious threat, and she doubted that it would be deterred without firepower.

"Thompson?" she asked gently. "Look at me, please. I need to know where I can find a map of this place."

He didn't respond. She sighed. There was no one home, although she did wonder briefly what was happening in his head.

***

His wife was snarling at him, her words nothing more than vicious, guttural growls. He could do nothing but cower from her twisted, plastic pastiche of a face. His child was there too, right beside her mother, a smug smile on her face. She was enjoying this, enjoying seeing him emasculated by this woman who had only married him for his money.

Little shit, he wanted to say. *I fucking gave you everything, you ungrateful fucking cunts!*

But he couldn't, not this time. His wife knew what to say, and it was hurting him. Each snarled word cutting straight to the bone. He felt tears running down his cheeks, heard himself whimper. Like some wounded dog, kicked into submission. All the fight had been stolen from him.

These women had ruined his life. Ripped away his manhood and torn it up in front of him as he begged and pleaded for mercy. But they had no mercy, just like his mother hadn't when she'd taken the belt to his cheeks, or slammed his head into a wall.

He was nothing. Neither man nor boy. Just a vessel to be used by whoever saw fit to do so. There wasn't a thing he could do about, because no matter how much money he had, or how good he looked, he was still that same little boy who couldn't assert his dominance.

What if you weren't?

It came from the blackness, eradicating the image of his twisted ex. His mother came into view, looking the same as he remembered, from when he was a child, years of rotting in a box having taken away nothing. Her long dark hair, perfect skin, loose-fitting summer dress.

The perfect wife, the perfect mother, how lucky he was to have her in his life, they would all say. His teachers, his friends, all believing the lies she put forward.

What if you weren't that little boy? she purred through her soft, ruby-red lips. *What if you were a man? Big and strong.*

She stepped forward, ran her fingers gently down his cheek. He'd never felt such a soft touch from her. Her soft hands had usually brought nothing but hurt.

I'm going to make you my big man. Her hands ran down his chest. *All you have to do is want it, as I have always wanted it. You will finally be the man I knew you could always be.*

He felt it then. It reared its head, worming up through the hate and disgust, a feeling for her he had not felt in a very long time. Love. A love for his mother, so pure and bright. But best of all, he felt it coming from her.

It feels good, doesn't it, big man? She smiled, perfect white teeth shining.

Thompson nodded. It did feel good. Better than his money. Or the sex he always paid for, where he couldn't feel powerful, no matter how rough he was. For the first time in a very long time, Bernard Thompson felt empowered. There was only one question that came to his mind.

His mother read his thoughts.

What will you do with this power, my big man?

22

They could hear it right behind them. Its claws skittered across the floor, the sound erratic. *The bullets that Anna had pumped into the creature had hurt it*, Jones thought. That was the only reason that they weren't already dead.

He'd regained his senses since the attack, but his arm was in pain. He could feel blood, warm and sticky, running down it. Anna was dragging him by his uninjured one, the gun gripped tightly in her other hand.

Adrenaline was driving her forward, just as it was with him. The corridor had a T-junction up ahead, and she dragged them left. Jones barely had time to register where they were before he was yanked to the right.

The young woman dragged them through an open door, closing it behind them as quickly and quietly as she could. She put her finger to her lips, eyes wide with fear, sweat pouring down her forehead and plastering her hair to her scalp.

Jones tried to steady his breathing, wincing as the full pain of his injury started to work its way through the adrenaline hit he'd just been given. He noticed Anna pointing frantically, and it took him a moment to remember the radio that was still gripped in his hand.

He nodded and raised it. Anna put her ear to the door, holding her finger up.

Wait.

Tic, tic, tic…

The sound stopped. An unnatural, guttural growl was heard on the other side of the door. Jones held his breath. Anna stood stock still.

Tic, tic, tic…

It stopped and growled again. Jones hoped he hadn't left a blood trail that would lead the thing right to them. If it burst through the door, he'd try and throw himself at it, give Anna a chance to get away.

His heartbeat sounded like a drumbeat in his ears. The rush of blood resembled a raging river. Jones was sure the creature could hear him, was convinced it was on the other side of the door, just waiting for the right moment to come in. It wasn't like doors could stop it—it had proved that when it had killed Eric.

After what seemed like an eternity, the creature growled again, and they heard its claws skittering across the floor away from them. Jones raised the radio to his lips. Anna nodded.

"Calder, Ekkow, anyone, come in. We need someone with a very big gun right fucking now."

"This is Calder, copy that. Where are you and how many of you are there?"

"It's just Anna and me. We encountered something. Eric is dead. We're in…" he looked around, "it looks like a room, but not for the guests. I'm guessing staff quarters? I don't know. We just took off running."

"Can you find anything in the room that might give us a clue?"

Anna nodded and began to search the small room. It was very utilitarian, just a bed set into the wall, a small table, wardrobe, and a door that presumably led to a bathroom. She went to the drawers first, pulling them open as quietly as she could. After a moment, she held up a book.

"There's a book in here. We got it from the drawer. Looks like a Terry Pratchett novel."

"Is there any…" Calder stopped. "Okay, we know where you are. Hang tight, we're coming."

"Axel, one more thing. Anna emptied an entire magazine into one of them. It didn't kill it, but it slowed it down."

"Good. If it gets injured, we can kill it."

***

"Is there any…" Calder started, about to ask if there was anything else that could identify the room, when Ekkow interrupted.

"That's my room, bruv."

"You read Pratchett?" Calder asked once he'd signed off.

"Hell yeah. That is some good writing."

Calder chuckled. "You're full of surprises."

"Um, guys," Billy said, "I don't mean to alarm you, but the slime stuff is getting closer."

The two soldiers got serious. "Okay, this is what we're gonna do. We know where Jones and Anna are, so we get them first. Then Ekkow, you and I are going to try to get them into a sub before we find Priya and Thompson. We clear?" The other two men nodded. "Good. Ekkow, you're on point, mate. Billy, you're in the middle. You do what we say, when we say. And if any fire fights break out, you get down, clear?"

Billy nodded. "I really don't want to die, man."

"You and me both, bruv," Ekkow said, readying his weapon.

***

"Never thought I'd actually miss home," Anna said as she pulled the torn bit of shirt tight around Jones' wound.

"Shit home life, huh?"

"Oh man, you have no idea. My dad's an ass."

"Aren't they all?"

Anna chuckled, sitting down on the floor and pulling her knees to her chest. "Asian kid problems. He doesn't show any affection, ships me off to events or parties or whatever. Guy only needs me around to show face. I mean, yeah, I get it, rich kid, tough life, all that shit. But still, man, sometimes I wonder, why the fuck did you have a kid if you didn't want to?"

"I don't know. My home life was pretty standard, I guess. My brother and I were close all our lives. None of that bullying stuff you get on TV. We just kind of got along from day one, never looked back."

"What happened to him?"

"He died," Jones said after a pause. "We both became journalists. He was embedded with a unit in Afghanistan. The official story is that an IED went off. You wanna know something funny? I always thought I'd be the one to bite it first. I mean, I was always taking the risks. He never did."

"I'm sorry to hear that, man. I have never had any siblings. My mother died when I was little, and my dad raised me with a collection of helpers and boarding schools. I guess I don't understand what it's really like to be close to someone like that."

"It's a good feeling. And since you saved my life back there, I guess we're going to get pretty tight. Although I realise you'd rather get close to Priya."

Anna's cheeks flushed. "How did you know?"

"It's pretty obvious, my dear."

"Fuck. Yeah, well, that's just another thing on my list of issues. Being gay in Singapore isn't exactly something that the society celebrates."

"Does your dad know?"

The young woman stifled a laugh. "Hell no. Not that he would care anyway, the *cheebai*."

"I guess we all have our secrets."

"Yeah. Fuck me, man, what the fuck are those things?"

"Don't think about them, we need to keep calm."

"How?"

"Do what we've been doing. Small talk, get to know each other. Something I learned being in military units the world over. You have to keep your mind off the shit to survive it."

"You think we will? Survive it, I mean."

Jones was quiet for a moment, looking into the girl's eyes. He could see the courage in them, but there was fear there too. It was to be expected. He was scared, and he'd been in the kind of situations most people only saw in movies. Whatever the fuck they were facing, it was unlike anything either of them had ever seen.

"We're going to try."

She smiled. "Thanks for being honest."

23

"Fuck," Priya said.

They'd been heading down a random corridor, hoping that they'd end up heading toward the med bay, but when they finally came upon a map on the wall, it was obvious that they weren't. They had been moving away from it.

It didn't help that progress was slow because of Thompson, who had now gone into an almost catatonic state. At least the man was willing to be led around, because there was no way she could bring herself to leave him behind.

Another thing had been bugging her for a while—the fact that they hadn't encountered any survivors. Nor had they come across any of the creatures. And yet she couldn't shake the feeling that she was being watched at every turn. There was a prickly feeling on the back of her neck, but every time she turned around, she saw nothing.

It was all getting a bit much. This job was supposed to have been easy, and fun. But now it was just a horror show. She was tired, the adrenalin having worn off and left an unbelievable tiredness in its place. It felt like her bones were aching. All Priya wanted to do was sit down.

She found herself doing it before she realised she was acting on the impulse. She shook her head and straightened. If they stopped, they'd die. She knew that as surely as she knew her name. And yet, the floor looked so inviting…

"Jesus Christ, girl, pull it together," she said out loud.

Thompson didn't react. He just stood there, staring off down the corridor.

What was he looking at?

Priya followed his gaze. About five metres ahead was a junction, shrouded in darkness. Which was weird, because she was sure that the emergency lighting had been on earlier…

She took a hesitant step forward, squinting down into the dark. It looked like there was something moving, but she couldn't be sure. Thompson had started whispering something under his breath, his words intelligible, but somehow they sent a chill down her spine.

Every instinct was telling her to turn and run. Tear down the corridor and not look back until she was far away. But common sense told her that that might not be the best idea. Instead, she gripped Thompson's hand and started slowly backing up, keeping her eye on the darkness.

There definitely was something hiding within it, although whether it was man or beast, she couldn't be sure. A coppery smell was emanating from the dark. Familiar, and somehow grotesque, it made her want to gag. And then, a voice.

"Help me…"

The words were strangely drawn out. They drifted through the empty space from out of the dark, reaching Priya's ears and sending goose pimples down her arms. It wasn't real, instead being as close to a voice as something that didn't have one could manage to make.

She continued to back up, her eyes locked on the thing she couldn't quite see. It continued to plead, to beg. The words making sense sometimes, and at others being nothing but gibberish. Thompson's eyes were locked on the same thing, his lips twisted into a strange, chilling smile.

Priya wanted to let go of the man's hand there and then. It took all her will power to keep it clamped around the rich man's wrist. Something about that smile was more terrifying than the thing in the dark.

A glance over her shoulder showed that the corridor wasn't as short as she'd thought. It seemed to stretch on endlessly, a long expanse of featureless, lifeless grey. In front of her, the darkness seemed to be advancing, tendrils of it inching forward, devouring the light as it went.

Terror more real than any she had ever felt gripped Priya's heart just then, its claws worming through her blood. It felt as if ice was slowly spreading through her body. She stopped moving without meaning to. Her legs just wouldn't obey.

"Help me…"

The voice that wasn't a voice was getting closer. Whatever was making it wasn't human. It wasn't of this world. And it was hungry. She could hear the hunger in the voice. The words were pleading, but the meaning behind them was clear. The thing was going to devour her, rip her very soul to shreds while she screamed. It was going to be a fate worse than death, and there was nothing she could do about it—all she could do was stand and watch it come.

Beside her, Thompson started to laugh. It started as a chuckle, before rising to a full-on belly-laugh. Tears streamed down his ashen face. His lips were pulled back in a dreadful mockery of a smile, flawless white teeth shining in the dim glow of the emergency lights.

But as suddenly as it began, the laughter stopped. The man stood upright and looked at what was coming, as if for the first time. His posture changed, from a man defeated to one that stood tall. Priya realised that whatever madness had gripped him was lifting, and she knew that this was their only chance.

"Run!" she screamed, yanking the man's arm and sprinting away.

As she'd hoped, the man followed suit, his dress shoes banging hard against the floor as they sprinted away. Behind them, the darkness continued to plead for help, drawing out the words as it did so, before it all became an unintelligible blur of nonsense.

***

There was a sudden wet, slurping sound, as if someone had just put their hand into a jar of slime. Calder spun round, his weapon up and ready. The black slime was working its way through the seams of the medical bay door, slowly oozing through the tiny crack it was making. The stuff was forcing itself through the door, eager to get to them.

"Oh fuck no," Billy said, backing away.

The stuff was moving faster than it had been, advancing upon them. Ekkow grabbed Billy by the shoulder and the three men backed slowly out of the room. Once they were clear, Calder sealed the door behind them.

"This stuff is everywhere," he said. "It was all over one of the corridors I took to get here. It calls to you."

Billy shivered. "And fucking attacks you, man. It got under my skin."

"So we stay away from it then," Ekkow said. He was tense, his shoulders tight. He rolled them a bit, working his muscles. "Bruv, I never thought I'd wish we were back in Afghanistan."

"Ekkow, we need to go. The sooner we round up the others, the sooner we get the fuck out of this place."

The big man nodded, but Calder noticed him barely supressing a shiver. With one last check of his shotgun, they started off. Billy fell in line behind him, obviously terrified. Sweat poured off his forehead, his pupils looked like big black saucers, and his movement was jerky, like a panicked rabbit. Calder made a note to keep an eye on him—that kind of terror made people unpredictable and irrational.

Calder had seen it too many times, watched good guys crack under pressure, and almost get themselves killed. Billy was just a civvie; he wasn't cut out for this kind of thing. Hell, if Calder was being honest, neither was he.

What the fuck were they even dealing with? An alien? Something from the depths of hell? It was absurd.

Calder shook his head. He had to keep his mind clear. People who got distracted in combat got dead.

He took a breath, centred himself. Whatever they were fighting, all that mattered was that it was trying to kill them. They didn't want to die. The rules were that simple. He had to compartmentalise. Same as he'd done in a hundred other dirty conflicts over the years. Us versus them—that was all that mattered.

24

"This look right to you?" Ekkow asked, stopping.

Billy and Calder stopped as well. Calder scanned the corridor in front of them. It was empty, featureless. The same as every other. Except…

"We should have been there by now," Calder said. "How long have we been walking?"

No one knew. Time had seemed to stretch on forever, and yet it had also seemed to pass in an instant. A paradox—like a car going backward and forward at the same time.

Billy was wringing his hands, his eyes darting nervously around. Sweat beaded his brow. Calder shared a look with Ekkow, who nodded. If he panicked, then they were fucked. Both men knew the risks of that a non-combatant posed in this type of situation.

"So, what do we do, bruv?"

Calder considered their options. Backward or forward. Two choices. Yet they had a mission, so there was only really one choice.

"We keep on. But we count steps, keep track of time. Make sure we're making progress."

Before going forward again, both Calder and Ekkow checked their watches and called out the time. Each man counted their steps as they moved. One pace, two, three, and on they went toward their destination.

Ten minutes later, they stopped. Time had passed, they had moved, and yet—it felt as if no progress had been made.

"It's playing with us," Billy whispered.

"What is?" Calder asked, but he knew the answer.

"Whatever we let in here. Whatever we woke up on the ocean floor."

"Why?"

"Because…because it can. It was in my head. I felt it learning, reading my thoughts, figuring me out. It felt as if it was laughing the whole time I cowered, the whole time I felt pain. The thing laughed."

Ekkow caught Calder's eye and shook his head. But Calder knew the man wasn't losing it. At least, not entirely. He could feel it all around them. A presence, alien, yes, but also intelligent. And he knew from long years of experience when he was being played with. How did the song go?

Despite all my rage, I am still just a rat in a cage…

"I don't think we can fight it, man. We just need to run. Get the fuck out of here and don't look back."

Billy started to babble, talking about escape, about leaving the others behind, finding a way out, destroying the place. Only half of it made sense, the rest was all desperate plans scratched out of an earth too dry to yield any fruit at all.

Calder tried to calm him. He spoke softly, earnestly, like he'd been trained. He knew how to deal with shock. After the man had finally calmed, Ekkow help up a hand, requesting silence.

Drip… Drip… Drip…

Calder nodded, spinning and aiming down the way they'd come. It sounded like someone had left a faucet on over a sink full of dishes. At regular intervals, a water droplet would fall onto a pot in the sink, making a metallic clink. And it was coming closer.

Drip… Drip… Drip…

Soon, it was joined by something else. A wet, slapping sound. It reminded Calder of when he went to the butcher as a kid, and the bloke would slap a steak down on the board after slicing it off.

Drip… Drip… Slap… Drip… Drip… Slap…

Billy was quiet, too scared to talk. His eyes bugged, his gaze switching from one end of the corridor to the other. Calder's hand tightened on his weapon, but he kept steady. He trusted Ekkow to do the same behind him. The two of them had been through hell together, working together as a unit. They trusted each other implicitly.

The sounds continued coming closer, the slapping picking up speed. Calder steadied his breathing, willing his heart to stop threatening to burst through his ribs. Whatever was coming would be greeted with lead.

"Eyes on!" Ekkow said, and then a second later, "Hold fire! Friendly contact."

Calder spun around, bringing his weapon to bear just in case, to find a sight he had never expected. At the end of the corridor stood Jackson, soaked in blood.

"Hello, boss."

25

"What the fuck?" Billy breathed.

Calder stared, his mind racing, his weapon pointed at a 45-degree angle toward the floor. It was Jackson. It just wasn't all of him.

The steady dripping continued, and the source was the ex-marine's left arm. It had been sheared off just above the elbow. The wound was jagged—a red mess of meat with a shiny white bone sticking out. Blood dripped from the wound in small, steady drops.

Jackson took a step forward, and Calder saw what the slapping sound had been. Because the step was more of a limp. The man's right foot had been ripped off at some point, leaving a messy stump of flesh behind, like he'd put his foot into a paper shredder.

The man was covered in dried blood, staining his combat uniform a dark crimson. A cut ran from just under his left eye to his jawline. His teeth seemed to be impossibly white in his smiling face.

"Hello, boss," Jackson said again.

There was something wrong about his smile. It was a grotesque parody of one, as if a puppet master had just pulled his skin into the best approximation of one. There was no humour in it. Calder's weapon rose another few degrees.

Jackson stepped forward.

Drip… Slap…

"I… think I need some help, boss."

"Stay there, bruv," Ekkow said, his shotgun aimed centre mass.

Calder's mind was blank. He had no idea what to do. His training was telling him to help. To rush forward and administer first aid. But his instincts were screaming at him.

Danger!

He brought his weapon up.

"Boss…" Jackson examined the stump of his arm, as if seeing it for the first time. "I should be in pain, shouldn't I?"

The man laughed—an empty sound that echoed through the silent hallway. He waved his bloody stump at them, taking another limping step forward.

"Stay put," Ekkow said, shotgun at the ready.

"There's something wrong with him, man," Billy said, trying to back away.

"Wrong?" Jackson stopped loping forward. "Nothing's wrong with me, boss."

"What happened?" Calder asked.

"I died." The man laughed. "I guess there is something wrong with me after all! I died in pain and alone, boss. Where were you?"

Calder said nothing.

Jackson smiled his parody smile. "There's something down here with us, boss. It chose you—all of you."

"Chose us for what?"

"I…don't know…"

Fluid started to leak from Jackson's eyes. The black goo flowed down his cheeks like viscous tears. His smile faded.

"It's in my head," he said. "Using me. It wants you all to know that you're going to die. Just like the others—the meat."

"Is that what it calls everyone else who died?"

"They were uninteresting." His speech was distorted now, the words stammering out of his mouth. "No. Not…like the others. Worse. They…were the lucky ones…"

More black liquid flowed out of Jackson, from his eyes, his ears, his mouth, his wounds. It pooled on the floor in front of him, a big sticky puddle as thick and black as fresh tar. The stench was unbelievable, a raw, stinging assault on the group's senses.

The black stuff finally stopped coming out of Jackson and shot backward, sliding across the floor away from the group. It disappeared around the corner, leaving Jackson standing, the steady dripping of blood from his ragged stump continuing.

The man's face went slack, and his good leg buckled. He hit the floor face first with a wet slap. Calder and Ekkow stood stunned, their weapons trained on nothing. Billy whimpered.

"This ain't normal, bruv. This shit just ain't fucking normal."

That's when they heard it. It was coming from behind them, a steady ticking, as if a dog's claws were skittering across tiles.

Ekkow and Calder spun round, Calder grabbing Billy and forcing him down, out of the line of fire. They started to back up, careful not to trip over Jackson's limp form. Billy continued to whimper, tears and snot running down his face.

"Whatever comes around that corner, take it out."

Ekkow nodded, focusing his sights on the empty corridor as the ticking continued. There was more than one thing coming. Calder could tell from the skittering.

"Multiple hostiles," he breathed, gripping Billy tightly, dragging the man back with him.

They were close now, almost in their line of sight. Calder steadied his breathing, gripped his weapon tight, preparing his arm for the recoil of the weapon. Ekkow did the same, getting the stock of the shotgun in the crook of his shoulder, ready to take the recoil.

The first creature came around the corner slowly. It had long, animal-like limbs, vicious claws, and razor-sharp teeth. Its body was pieced together from human flesh. Great chunks of it, torn into ragged strips and stitched onto itself. Calder noticed an ear on its chest, and what looked like the flesh of a face that had been flayed off the skull, the eye holes and mouth revealing pulsating black flesh underneath it.

All of this occurred to him in seconds, but he forced his brain not to think. He didn't have time to think, and if he could have comprehended what was in front of him, he'd have gone mad. So, he fired.

Two shots flew straight and true. The rounds hit the creature in what Calder assumed was its chest. It howled in pain and anger, its eyes locking onto the three men. Then there was the deafening boom of the shotgun as Ekkow pulled his trigger.

Half of the creature's head disappeared in a mess of red and black blood, and it was flung backward. Calder turned his attention to the second one, aiming for the head, his rounds hitting their mark.

Ekkow fired again, this shot taking a limb off of a second creature. But it kept coming, crawling over the floor, its movements graceful and grotesque all at once. Calder shoved Billy behind him and took up a two-handed stance, emptying the rest of his magazine into the on-coming threat.

"Reloading," he said, dropping the spent mag and sliding a fresh one home.

A third creature appeared, ragged flesh stretched and stitched over its awful form. It paid no mind to its twitching brethren, instead advancing forward. Calder put his rounds into its head, squeezing off shot after shot.

Ekkow fired a couple more times and slung his weapon over his shoulder while drawing his pistol from its holster, all in one smooth movement.

"We need to leave," Calder said, putting more rounds on-target.

The three men started to retreat, firing as they went, the shell casings bouncing off the wall and hitting the floor. The three creatures kept coming. Even the one with only half a head, its ragged wound leaking black fluid. They screamed as they came, an unholy, inhuman cry.

"Once we get around that corner," Calder shouted over the deafening gunfire, hoping Billy and Ekkow were hearing him, "we fucking leg it!"

They kept moving back until they reached the junction, and Calder pushed Billy forward, yelling at him to run. They took off, Billy stumbling at first, but he found his feet soon enough. Behind them, the creatures continued to scream. The thumping of their boots was joined by the sound of skittering claws, and then the laughter started.

Jackson's laugh. It echoed from everywhere and nowhere at once, following them as they ran. Calder risked a look over his shoulder, seeing the things coming closer.

"Kitchen!" he yelled.

Ekkow acknowledged. The kitchen had fire doors—strong sturdy ones that could lock in the event something went wrong. Calder hoped that they would keep the creatures out.

They continued to run, their lungs burning, sweat pouring off of them. Billy was flagging, the skinny man nowhere near the level of fitness of the two soldiers. Ekkow grabbed his shoulder, pulling him along as they went. It wasn't far now, just one more turn.

They careened around the corner, and Calder heard a screech behind him. He glanced back to see a creature sail past his field of vision. If they hadn't have turned, it would have landed on their backs. It hit the wall with a thud, unable to stop itself. A scream of frustration escaped its mouth.

Then they were through the door. Ekkow threw Billy forward. He crashed into a countertop, sending pots and pans clattering everywhere. Calder ignored him, instead spinning around and slamming the doors shut. Ekkow helped him bolt them, and they both braced themselves against the doors.

They waited, breathing hard. It didn't take long for the doors to rattle as the creatures threw themselves into them.

Thud.

Thud.

But the doors barely moved and after another couple of attempts, they heard more screams of frustration, and then the sound of skittering claws retreating.

Calder looked to Ekkow, both of them soaked in sweat and breathing hard.

"Fuck me sideways."

26

Priya had no idea where they were. They'd just sprinted away from the darkness, blindly taking corners wherever they could. There had only been one objective—escape. And now they were paying the price for it.

Thompson didn't know where he was either, even though he was more together than he had been in a while. He wasn't totally out of it anymore, but he wasn't all there either. He kept casting glances in Priya's direction when he thought she wasn't looking. It was getting disturbing.

Finally, the featureless grey gave way to plush carpets as they pushed through a door into a huge casino. Slot machines, roulette tables, poker tables—the place was fully equipped, and she even spied a bar at the other end of the room. Overhead was another glass dome, showing nothing but the darkness of the ocean outside.

"Fuck it," Priya said after a moment of deliberation, heading straight for the bar.

She hopped over it, selected a fine bottle of bourbon, pulled the cap off, and chugged it straight from the bottle. The burn felt good as the alcohol slid its way down her throat.

She offered the bottle to Thompson. "Want some?"

He shook his head. Shrugging, she took another pull.

"How's your dream feeling now?" she asked.

"What?"

"All of this is your dream, isn't it? And now it's soaked in blood. How does it feel?"

He looked at her strangely. "You talk as if I wanted this."

"Two men died before this project was finished. Most people would have taken that as a sign."

"That wasn't my fault. I searched for them. How do you even know that?"

"I'm a journalist. I do my research."

"You just want to destroy me, don't you?"

His eyes had taken on an odd sheen, the veins on his neck popping as his muscles tensed. Priya took a step back, thankful that the bar was between them.

"You're destroying yourself, Thompson. You think this place can open after all of this? It's finished. And you don't seem to care."

"Of course I care!" he said, snarling. "My friends died out there!"

"Were they friends? Or bags of money with legs?"

"You bitch. You're just like all the rest. Fucking cunts, all of you. You just want to destroy me." His hands were on the bar now. "All this fucking *Me Too* shit. All because *women* like you want to destroy successful men."

Priya knew she should have been worried, or at least a little scared. But she wasn't. She'd met men like Thompson before. Men who thought women were nothing more than objects. And after all she had seen this day, this man didn't scare her.

"We're not trying to destroy you. You're perfectly capable of doing that all by yourself."

"I could kill you, you know," he said, very calmly. "No one would know."

There was something about the way he said it that chilled the blood in her veins. So she smashed the half-empty bottle of bourbon across the side of his head.

27

"You think they're still coming?" Anna asked.

Jones' side had really started to hurt, the pain seemingly getting worse with each breath. Each inhale was a blade stabbing straight into his ribs. He was trying his best to hide his grimaces. They had already tried the radio.

"Honestly? I think they ran into some trouble. Those things are probably everywhere."

"So, what do we do?"

Jones thought about it. The Kingdom was probably crawling with those creatures by now, and they were pretty much canned goods at the moment. They were hidden for now, but if one of those things found them, there was no escape.

"Well, we have two options: Stay here and wait for rescue, or head out and look for a way out."

"Both are equally as bad as each other, aren't they?"

Jones nodded. "I'm not going to lie, yes, they are. But I really do think that Calder got waylaid by something. Priya is out there somewhere, and I want to find her."

"You're not leaving me here while you go poking around," Anna said, reading his thoughts. "You are way too badly injured to go it alone, and I'm not some fucking damsel in distress. What we need to do is link up with the others."

"I guess the choice is made then."

"You're not going to argue with me?"

"It wouldn't do any good. Besides, I'm pretty damn sure nowhere in this fucking place is safe."

They didn't have much in the way of weapons. One empty sidearm and a tactical knife did not an arsenal make, but they had no other choices.

Anna suggested that they first find a map on one of the walls, and see if they could head in the direction of the submarine bay, while trying the radio intermittently to let Calder know where they were. In the absence of good plans, Jones agreed it was the best they had.

They started by cracking the door. Jones peeked out, listened, and then went out into the corridor. Looked left, then right, listened again, then motioned Anna out.

They crept down the corridor, each step bringing waves of pain shooting through Jones' side. He bit down hard, stifling his cries into grunts. There was a T-junction up ahead. *Left or right?*

Knowing the general direction of the submarine bay, Jones turned left, and stopped dead. Standing in front of him was his brother.

"Hey, bro," Eugene said.

He was wearing his desert BDUs. Dust covered him, parts of his uniform ripped to shreds. There was a horrifying, ragged, gaping hole in his side, exposing some of his organs. Half of his face was a bloody mess. His brain was exposed, a slimy pink mass that throbbed and undulated. One good eye stared back at Jones, full of the life and sparkle that Eugene always used to have.

"Sorry about the mess," Eugene said with a grotesque half-smile. "IEDs will do that to ya. What's the matter, bro? You don't want to give your brother a hug?"

The *thing* in front of him raised its hands and stepped forward. Jones stared, his mouth agape, his mind trying to make sense of what he was seeing.

"Come on, bro. I know I look different, but it's still me. Remember when we used to wrestle as kids? I'd always lose, and you'd tell me that I'd get you next time. But I never did. We were supposed to sort it out when I got back from Afghan."

"What the fuck are you?"

"I'm Eugene."

"No," Jones declared, stepping back. "My brother is dead. He died in Afghanistan when an IED went off next to his vehicle."

"I never said I wasn't dead." The smile again. "Death is just a different state of being, bro."

"Jones, we have to go." Anna was tugging his arm, trying to get him to move.

"You should try it, bro. I mean, I can do this now."

Eugene reached into his gaping wound and fished around. There was a terrible, wet squelching sound as he did so.

"Ah." He pulled out his heart, still beating and bloody. He held it out. "I give you my heart, bro."

He started to laugh. It came from everywhere and nowhere, echoing down the corridor. Jones stared at his brother's beating heart as it leaked fluids onto the floor. Bile rose in his throat.

"What's the matter? You don't want something that comes from my heart. I tell you what—you take mine, and I'll take yours."

Jones stumbled backward, Anna dragging him as best she could.

"Run!" She was screaming, the words barely penetrating Jones' stupor.

Finally, his legs obeyed, and they were half-running, half-stumbling away from the laughing figure.

"I'll get it later, bro. Don't you worry!"

***

"Did you see any of them go down?" Calder asked. Billy and Ekkow shook their heads. "Fuck. Neither did I."

"I know they got hurt. And I blew off a couple of limbs for sure. But I have no idea if the fuckers actually stayed down."

"There were just so fucking many of them," Billy said. "So fucking many."

"Best case, there are a few less now. Worst case, we did nothing."

"Bruv, we need better weapons."

"Like a fucking rocket launcher," Billy said.

Calder stared at him. "In a sardine can at the bottom of the ocean, you want us to use a rocket launcher?"

"Oh. Right. Fuck. I should never have taken this fucking job, man."

"Ekkow is right. We need more weapons, more ammo. So we need to head to the armoury."

"What's the plan, boss? Throw everything at them and see what works?"

"Not like we have any other options, mate."

A pot clanged hard as it hit the floor. Calder and Ekkow had their weapons up almost immediately. That's when they heard it. The clicking of claws above their heads.

"Fuck, fuck, fuck," Billy breathed.

The two security officers remained silent, their eyes trained on where the clicking was coming from. It sounded like the thing was crawling along in the ceiling. Every now and then, it would stop to scratch around a bit. It was looking for a weak point, Calder knew.

While the walls were thick steel, he wondered about the ceiling. Air vents, pipes, all kinds of things were up there—which meant that there was nothing but a thin bit of metal between them and the creature.

Ekkow motioned behind him with his shoulder, a silent question. Calder shook his head. It was too dangerous to go back the way they came. He attracted Billy's attention and pointed to the door at the other end of the rectangular room.

A steel workbench separated the space, and Calder motioned Ekkow left so that he could take right. Billy followed Ekkow.

Their eyes and weapons aimed upward, they started forward. The military men walked silently, rolling their feet with each step to minimise noise. Billy was slightly less quiet, but only just. His breathing was ragged, coming in short, sharp breaths.

The creature continued to move around above them, its dreadful claws making ear-piercing screeching sounds as it dragged them across the metal above. The three men moved slowly, agonising over each step, each wanting to just sprint for the door in front of them.

It seemed so far away. And they had no idea what could be waiting for them behind the door. The options ran through Calder's mind, but he pushed them back, refusing to assume or make up scenarios. They would deal with whatever was behind the door when they came to it.

And that's when the door in front of them burst open, swinging inward and clanging into the hard steel wall with a terrific crash.

28

Several things happened at once.

Billy let out a surprised yell. Ekkow and Calder brought their weapons down to aim at the door. Jones and Anna stopped dead in their tracks at the sight of the gun barrels aimed in their direction.

And the ceiling fell apart behind Calder.

He spun to see one of the creatures landing in the middle of a shower of splintered metal. Training took over and he put two bullets into the creature's face before he had time to think.

Ekkow joined in the fight with his shotgun. A deafening blast sent buckshot ripping into the thing's stolen flesh, sending pieces and black goo flying. As the big man racked another shell into the chamber, the creature's arm moved.

It took a moment for Ekkow to register what had just happened. The thing's arm had blurred, and suddenly there was a sharp pain in his right arm. He felt blood—hot, wet, sticky—rolling down his forearm. He looked to see a jagged piece of metal sticking out of the meat of his arm.

Ekkow's finger twitched on the trigger as the pain travelled to his brain. The blast from the shotgun knocked the weapon out of his weakened hand and ignited something flammable.

Calder watched as the creature was suddenly engulfed in flames, its piercing shrieks causing him to stumble back and protect his ears. And then something amazing happened.

The thing fell to its knees, and after a few moments, the shrieks died away as it continued to burn.

"Fire," Calder breathed. "We need to burn the fuckers."

"Calder!" Billy called.

Billy was crouched next to Ekkow, trying to keep him from moving his arm. Calder leaped over the table.

"Jesus Christ, bruv, this hurts," Ekkow said.

"Don't fucking touch it, mate. Billy! Find some whiskey, there has to be some in here somewhere. Jones, get over here, help me get him up. Anna, grab the shotgun. We need to move now!"

Everyone rushed to do as they were told, too stunned by everything that had just happened to argue. Both Ekkow and Jones grunted as the big man was lifted up.

"You okay, Jones?"

"Yeah, fine."

"Then let's get the fuck out of here."

More skittering of claws urged them on. The doors behind them started to shudder as the things attacked them with renewed vigour. Ekkow shrugged out of the grip of the two men, saying he was fine to run.

"Where to?"

"Casino!" Calder yelled, glancing back over his shoulder. "We can barricade the door."

Anna struggled under the weight of the shotgun, so Jones grabbed it from her. He racked a shell into the chamber and fired. Something screamed, but Calder kept moving.

Ekkow was falling behind, his injured arm leaving a trail of blood behind him. His vision was starting to blur. He stumbled, but Anna just barely caught him, urging him on by pushing him from behind.

"Covering!" Calder yelled, spinning and drawing his weapon in one smooth movement.

Rounds tore into their pursuers as everyone rushed past, slowing the creatures down. Calder ejected his spent magazine and continued to run. Billy was leading the way, the bottle of whiskey clutched tightly in his hand.

Jones' side felt like it was on fire, each ragged breath bringing a wave of pain through his body. Stars blossomed in front of his eyes. More gunfire as Calder tried again to push the things back.

Jones turned, racked a fresh shell, and fired again, not even able to aim. He was rewarded with another frustrated screech. He racked, pulled the trigger, and...

Click.

He swore. The chamber was empty.

"Move!" Calder yelled and Jones started running again, his pace slowing with each step.

Ekkow wasn't much better off. He was losing blood and fast. He was contemplating giving up when the doors leading to the casino came into view. Expertly carved, perfectly varnished mahogany double doors stood wide open, inviting them into a world of slot machines, tables, and alcohol.

Billy was through first, urging the others on as he stood aside. They piled in, Billy and Anna slamming the big doors shut behind them.

"Fuck, fuck, fuck," Billy exclaimed, leaning against the doors and taking a swig of whiskey.

"Billy, get to the bar," Calder said. "I want you to open every bottle they have. Anna, there should be a first-aid kit there as well—find it. Jones, watch the door. Ekkow, with me."

Everyone rushed to do their tasks. Jones took some shells out of Ekkow's pocket and reloaded the shotgun. Calder sat the big man down with his back against the bar. He pulled off his belt and used it as a makeshift tourniquet, pulling it as tight as he could and giving the free end to Ekkow.

"Bite on this, mate," he said, putting it in his mouth. "Anna, I need that kit."

"Here!"

Calder opened the kit. He pulled out the surgical alcohol and poured it over the wound on Ekkow's arm. He checked to make sure that the jagged piece of metal hadn't gone straight through his friend's arm.

"Looks like it's just in the meat, mate."

"Doesn't feel like it," Ekkow said through the belt.

"Well, we gotta get it out."

He poured the alcohol all over his hands, rubbing them vigorously together, before finding a pair of latex gloves in the kit. He snapped them on, gave Ekkow a nod, and then slowly extracted the shrapnel. Ekkow gritted his teeth hard, the leather rubbing uncomfortably against them. As the thing came out with a sickening wet squelching, blood started to pour out of the wound.

"Okay, now the hard part."

Calder wiped the wound down and pulled out what looked like a needle from the kit. He poured more alcohol over it and splashed some more over Ekkow's wound. Ignoring the big man's grunt, he pulled surgical thread out of the pack, threaded the needle, and slowly, painstakingly started stitching the gash closed.

Ekkow bit down hard on the belt, his teeth almost going right through the thick, brown leather. Each stab of the needle sent a wave of pain shooting up his arm. Drool came out the sides of his mouth, and his eyes watered.

"Okay, hard part done."

"So soon?" Ekkow quipped.

The last of the alcohol went over the stitches before Calder put gauze on it and wrapped it tight with a bandage.

"Calder," Jones called, "it looks like the bastards are going to break down this door!"

"Fuck. Anna, Billy. Find some towels! Soak them in alcohol and start stuffing them into the bottles!"

"Really, bruv? Molotovs in an underwater hotel?"

"I know, mate, but it's the only way to stop those damn things. And I'm hoping the fire system will kick in once they're dead. State of the art tech, remember?"

Ekkow flexed the fingers on his injured hand. "Well, if we die, at least we die fighting."

"And on fire," Anna quipped.

Calder grinned. The doors rattled again.

"Jones, get over here. Anna, Billy, hunker down behind the bar. Here," Calder handed them a lighter, "when I say, light the towels and pass the bottles to us."

The three men readied their weapons. The doors rattled again as something banged into them. Cracks started to appear in the well-varnished wood. Calder knew it would only take a couple more hits. He was about to ask Anna for a Molotov when the doors suddenly flew inward. The one on the left flew off its hinges and crashed into a slot machine, sending glass and coins flying.

But what stood in the door frame wasn't a group of feral monstrosities. It was, in fact, an entirely different kind of horror.

It was Eugene Jones.

"Hello, Axel."

29

Priya's mad run had taken her down multiple corridors. Corridors that had become warped visions of their former selves. She had even lost her camera somewhere along the way.

The carpet under her feet, once plush and expensive, squelched uncomfortably with each timid step she took. She didn't dare too look what had soaked into it to make it that way, but it did not stop her mind conjuring up horrifying images.

Even the walls offered no solace. Their once-polished mahogany texture had been twisted here and there with thick vestibules of flesh that pulsated like the arteries of some grotesque creature. Something thick, black, and viscous dripped from the ceiling from yet more of the strange flesh that seemed to run throughout this part of The Kingdom.

Some horrifying force pulled Priya forward, when all she wanted was to turn and flee. At this point, even the crushing blackness of the deep sea was preferable.

Ahead, the corridor split off in two different directions. The wall in front of her had something *in* it. She could barely make it out in the dim light, but it looked as if something was tangled within the weird tentacles. Two parts of it were moving, and a strange groaning sound could be heard.

Step by agonising step, Priya advanced. The things in the walls seemed to react to her presence, pulsing faster as she passed, and then calming when she was out of range. The groaning was getting louder. To her sheer, unimaginable horror, she realised that it was human.

Hhhhhhhhhhelppppppp…

A bizarre glow suddenly appeared, as if from nowhere, giving Priya a good look at the thing in the wall. She gasped, holding her hand over her mouth and clenching her jaw shut to stem the rising tide of vomit that threatened to burst from her lips.

The thing in the wall had once been human, but it was not one anymore. In fact, it looked like multiple people had been moulded together, as if their skin was as malleable as clay. Five different coloured eyes stared back at Priya, glistening and leaking pus. A mouth that seemed to have several sets of teeth opened, emitting that awful groan. Hands that seemed to be made of different skin tones clutched at her and she got the feeling that they were reaching out for aid.

Finally, she could hold it no longer, and the bile spewed from her mouth. Her vomit mixed with the liquid on the carpet, creating an icky yellowish, black liquid that soaked into further into the once-plush threads.

Once she had finally stemmed the flow of puke, Priya stood up shakily. The creature in the wall still reached for her, and she realised with horror that there were more things like it melded into the walls further down.

She pulled out her phone, thankful that she still had battery left, and opened her camera app. She was a journalist, and she had a job to do. People needed to know about this—even if it killed her.

***

Thompson watched her flee, taking pleasure in her fear. He saw it all clearly now—this was a gift. Being down here, in his Kingdom. Everything that was happening was good for him, not bad. Because he finally felt free.

"My special man," his mother said, standing in front of him, a smile across her pretty face. "I did this for you. All of this."

He nodded. She was more beautiful than he remembered. His last memories of her were vague at best. Fragments of memories fading into nothing in his head. Yet, here she was. In his world. Making things better for him.

She held out her hand, and he took it gladly, following her as they moved through the corridors toward the ballroom. Where it had all started.

His dreams of the ballroom were what had inspired him to create The Kingdom. If only he'd known how beautiful it would become.

As they moved, he noticed the walls change. But even they were lovely to his eyes. He saw no death and horror. He saw freedom and smiles—hands reaching out to touch the man who had made it all possible.

He stood tall then, for he knew that he had saved these people. Saved them from their dreadful, meaningless existence. They had become a part of his vision and they were finally happy. Their moans of pleasure were a testament to that.

They came upon the doors to the ballroom and his mother turned to him. She took his face in her gentle, soft hands, leaning in close. He could smell the shampoo in her hair as she put her lips to his and kissed him.

His eyes closed as he lost himself in the ecstasy of the moment. Her tongue snaked through his lips, forcing his mouth open. It was in his mouth, moving deeper. But it did not stop.

It kept going, worming its way down his throat. He gagged, struggling to breathe, as it went down his windpipe, forcing its way deeper and deeper. Soon it was in his lungs, filling them, expanding them.

Blood poured out of his nose as his body started to spasm. The blood soon gave way to an inky-black substance. It came out of his ears and forced his eyes out of their sockets until there were hanging by their stems, meaning that he never saw the creature kissing him for what it was.

Those trapped in the walls still moaned for help, their bizarre, misshapen hands reaching out, but getting nothing but air, as something resembling tears streamed from their eyes.

And yet, as all of this happened, and the empty husk once known as Thompson was filled with the creature, his brain told his body that he was in intense ecstasy, and the smile never once left his face.

30

"Eugene… What the fuck?" was all Calder could say.

Everyone stood frozen, staring at the mess in front of them. Dark droplets of blood still dripped to the floor steadily, hitting it with an impossibly loud splash in the silence of the casino.

"That's not your brother, Jones!" Anna shouted.

She vaulted over the bar and ran to him, grabbing him by the arm. Calder couldn't decide what to do, his mind refusing to make sense of what was before him. Billy stood motionless. Ekkow had his weapon aimed at the thing's head.

Jones just stared, his weapon hanging at a 45-degree angle, unsure whether to raise or lower it.

"Ekkow!" the thing said with a smile. "I missed you, big man! What? You didn't think I forgot about you, did ya?"

The thing laughed. Anna was shaking Jones now, desperately trying to get him to listen.

"This isn't your brother! It's something else, can't you see it? It's an illusion."

"Come on, guys, are you gonna listen to this little dyke cunt? It's me. I mean, I know I'm a little the worse for wear," he said, reaching into his chest cavity experimentally, "but it's still me. Well, mostly anyway."

Jones and Calder lowered their weapons, transfixed by the thing they were seeing. Their minds were rebelling, trying desperately to make sense of what was in front of them. Anna waved her hand in front of Jones' face and got no response.

"Jesus fucking Christ," she screamed, wrenching the shotgun from the man's limp grip. "Hey, arsehole, shut the fuck up!"

And with that she fired. She didn't account for the kickback and was knocked backward. But she was close enough that it didn't matter. Eugene's arm was blown clean off in an impressive spray of blackish, pulpy gore.

The Eugene thing looked at his mutilated arm. It squirmed and writhed on the floor behind him.

"Huh. Didn't expect that. Well, it looks like I'll just have to do this the old fashioned way."

As he spoke, his voice morphed from Eugene's into something else. Something hollow and empty, and yet threatening. An alien sound that didn't come from vocal cords. The flesh that covered the thing started to peel off, slopping to the floor and landing with a horrible, wet slapping sound. As it fell, it became clear that it wasn't all the same colour, and was instead an amalgamation of different skin tones horribly stitched into one.

What was underneath was even more horrifying. Undulating black, glistening skin, through which weird, alien organs could be seen pulsating. The shape of the thing was indescribable, as it seemed to be one shape and many all at once.

A horrible groaning sound was coming from it, rising in pitch until it became an ear-splitting screech that caused those present to put their hands over their ears.

Calder collapsed to his knees, a yell of pain escaping his lips as the creature continued to assault his senses. Jones struggled to get to Anna, stumbling as he went. Blood started to trickle from his ears.

Ekkow still stood, a grimace of intense pain on his face. He was pulling the trigger of his weapon, the rounds going wide as his aim wavered erratically. Eventually, he ran out of bullets and stumbled backward, falling against the bar.

The pain from the impact of the bar shook some sense into him and he grabbed a Molotov, fishing a lighter from his pocket. As his eyes and ears leaked blood, he managed to light it with shaking hands and toss it with all his might.

The bottle fell just short. It shattered on impact, throwing flaming liquid onto the creature. Its scream changed tones as it reacted to the fire, and suddenly the onslaught to everyone's senses stopped.

"Move!" Ekkow screamed at the top of his voice.

Calder snapped to his senses and struggled to his feet. Jones grabbed Anna's hand and hoisted her up, taking the shotgun from her as he did so.

"Run!" he shouted, cocking a fresh shell into the chamber and advancing toward the screaming creature.

"No!" Anna screamed as Jones fired, her pleas lost in the booming report of the weapon.

Calder grabbed her, pulling her with him toward the exit. Ekkow and Billy were already heading there, each carrying as many Molotovs as they could.

They burst through the doors, Calder pushing Anna ahead of him and making to go back for Jones. Ekkow grabbed him before he could do so.

"Bruv, we need to move now!"

"I need to go back and get him."

Ekkow slammed the doors shut. "Just move, you stupid bastard!"

Jones racked another shell into the weapon and fired. He continued to do so until he heard the hollow click of a dry chamber.

"How the fuck did you get my brother's image?" he screamed, tears and snot running down his face. "Tell me, you fucking son of a bitch!"

Suddenly, an appendage whipped toward Jones and into his chest. He let out a gasp, as a white-hot stab of pain ripped through his body. The thing withdrew, agonisingly slowly, making a disgusting wet sucking sound as it did so, bringing something up in front of his face. His own bleeding heart was held up to his dying eyes.

"I told you I'd get your heart, bro," the thing said, letting out a burst of inhuman laughter as Jones fell to the floor, twitching.

31

"Jesus," Billy said, panting, sweat pouring off his forehead.

Calder has no idea where they were. Their mad dash had led them into a room where pulsating, translucent, black things snaked their way into and out of the walls. At various points were people—or rather what was left of them—their dead hands clutching in vain at empty air.

"Today is a really bad fucking day," Ekkow said, clutching at his arm. The bandages had soaked through with blood.

A chorus of hideous, low moans echoed through the room, as the people in the walls called to the newcomers. Calder moved to get a closer look, but Anna pulled him back.

"We need to stay away from them," she said, tears in her eyes. "I think if we get too close, we could end up like them."

Calder nodded, cursing himself for being so stupid. "Okay. You heard the lady—stay away from the walls. We need to find Priya and get the fuck out of here."

There was something else wrong with the room they were in, besides the obvious. Something was nagging at him, jumping up and down in his peripheral vision, trying to get him to pay attention, but he couldn't figure out what it was.

They moved forward slowly, trying not to look at the people fused into the walls, trying to block out their whispered cries, but failing on both counts. Their feet splashed as they walked, the water soaking into the hems of their trousers.

That's when Calder realised what was wrong.

"We're standing—" he started.

"—in water," Anna finished.

"Fuck's sake, man," Billy said. "These tentacles things must have cracked the structure somehow."

He bent and checked the depth of the water.

"How long do we have before the whole place is flooded?" Ekkow asked.

"No way to tell. But I'm guessing we're on the fucking clock here. Seriously, fuck this job and fuck Thompson."

"So we hurry up then," Anna said firmly.

Calder glanced at her, a smile on his face. "Again, the lady is right. Nothing we can do. We keep moving."

"But where? We have no idea where the woman is!" Billy said.

"I saw some smashed glass near the bar earlier," Ekkow said. "Almost cut my hand open on the stuff when I stood. Someone was there before us. And stands to reason, if she was with Thompson, they'd make their way to the ballroom and then to the submarine bay."

"I guess we have a plan then. Anna, Billy, stay in front of me. Ekkow, take point. Move fast, but keep your eyes peeled. We don't know what else we're going to run into."

As they moved through the twisted, misshapen halls, things seemed to get worse. The ceiling dripped a weird, viscous substance that soaked into the floor, there seemed to be more tentacles than actual wall, and more people were fused into the stuff, although they were getting progressively more spread out, as if someone had tried to make too little wallpaper stretch onto too much wall.

The group tried their best to breathe through their noses, as the alien stench that was something of a combination of brine, rot, blood, and other even less savoury smells threatened to suffocate them. Even now and then, Anna would glance around, praying that she didn't see Priya's face in one of the walls.

"I have a bad feeling, bruv," Ekkow said, stopping.

"It's getting worse, isn't it?" Anna asked.

Calder nodded, glancing back over his shoulder. "I doubt she'd come this way if it's this bad."

"But didn't you notice?" Anna said. "Whatever this stuff is, it has blocked off all the side corridors."

"We're being funnelled to the ballroom."

"What are you thinking, bruv?"

Calder stared at the thing in the wall. "I'm thinking that it's possible that whatever this stuff is, it belongs to one entity. Think about it. All the things that have been happening, Eugene, the walls, the hallucinations, it's all had *some* kind of purpose behind it. Some kind of intelligence. Even the corridors."

"So whatever it is, it's in the ballroom?" Anna breathed. "So, we go back? Find another way?"

"Can't," Calder said simply. "We're blocked off behind us too. I noticed the tentacle things moving earlier. We have one way forward."

"Can't we burn ourselves an exit?" Ekkow asked.

"Too risky. We only have four Molotovs. And I think we're going to need it for whatever is behind this."

"This is insane, man," Billy said. "Fucking black sludge with a brain? Do you fucking hear yourselves? This isn't a movie."

"I didn't say it had a brain. I said it was intelligent. The point is moot anyway. We only have one choice. Even if we could burn ourselves one exit, I think the thing will just block off another path."

"We keep going then," Anna said. "And just pray Priya is there."

***

Priya knelt beside the shredded, bloodied clothes in front of her. It was a security uniform, as far as she could tell, and if she was lucky…

"Yes!" she exclaimed, pulling a handgun from under what was once a man's jacket.

She checked the magazine, discovering to her great relief that it was full. Sliding it back into the weapon, she checked that the safety was on, before standing up again. She had been wandering the ghastly halls for a while now, documenting what she could.

What was weird was that she hadn't run into any creatures or survivors. The Kingdom appeared deserted. She even seemed to be moving away from whatever had melded itself with the walls.

Not that it helped her at all, considering she had no idea where she was. She swore, looking around her, despairing at her situation.

"I'm tired, I'm scared, and I just want to get the fuck out of this place," she said out loud.

Nothing answered her. She really was all alone. Her eyes started to sting. The tears were threatening to flow. Her father had always told her not to cry, but her grandmother had taken her aside one day and told her that it was okay.

"Cry it out, child. Go somewhere quiet, where you can be alone. Cry all you want. But when you're done, you stand up tall, and you keep going."

So she cried. For a few brief moments, Priya let it all out. The loneliness, the frustration, the fear, the worry. She sobbed, her shoulders racking, her chest heaving, snot and tears running down her face and staining her clothes.

Then she stopped. She steadied her breathing and stood tall. It wasn't fair. People had died, she didn't know if she was going to survive, and she was all alone. But life wasn't fair. So she put one foot in front of the other and started moving. If she was going to die, she was going to die fighting.

In front of her, by some miracle not obscured or damaged by the rot that invaded the rest of the station, was a sign with an arrow pointing toward a set of stairs. It read "Ballroom."

Priya heaved a sigh of relief. From there, it would be a straight shot to the submarine bay and freedom. All she could do was hope that Calder and the others were waiting for her there. It was only a sliver of hope, but it was enough to spur her forward.

From the walls, dead eyes watched her pass. Somewhere inside their heads, what was left of their human selves wished for death.

32

"Okay, this is it. Ekkow, check your ammo," Calder said. "Anna, Billy, you hang onto those Molotovs, okay? Wait for my say so before using them. And stay behind Ekkow and me."

They nodded. Calder checked his magazine. It was his second to last; Ekkow was on his third to last. He had a feeling that whatever was behind the doors to the ballroom in front of them was going to need more than that. But they were out of options.

He had noticed that the black slime that Billy had talked about was creeping down the corridor toward them, almost imperceptibly. Something wanted them to meet it. And whatever it was had killed people, fucked with their minds, and herded them here like cattle.

Calder could almost feel the power radiating from behind that door. His skin crawled, his hair standing on end. The others had noticed it too. There was a feeling of unease shared by all of them. Their hearts were beating faster, and it felt like something was trying to work its way into their heads.

The force was pushing on their consciousness, causing all of them to experience the worst migraine they had ever had. It was almost blinding. Calder's head throbbed, sweat beading on his forehead. He didn't even know if he could still put rounds on target.

"Ready?" he asked, putting his hand to the door.

Everyone nodded. He took a breath, turned the handle, and pushed the door inward. He and Ekkow went in first, weapons up and ready. They were the first to see the unimaginable horror on the other side.

The first thing they noticed was the overwhelming coppery stench of blood, followed soon after by what could only be described as the very essence of rot. It assaulted their noses, almost causing them to gag.

Next came the almost indescribable horror of the scene before them. Bodies, or bits of bodies, were scattered everywhere in great piles that heaved every now and then as things moved among the dead.

Blood coated the floor, making it slick and dark brown. Snaking tentacles of the black substance weaved their way in and out among the pieces of the dead, spreading out to the walls from a central mass in the middle of the ballroom.

Calder couldn't comprehend what it was. It had no shape that could be described by human eyes, and seemed to change and morph as he looked at it. It was huge, reaching almost to the domed ceiling, and made up of some translucent, slimy black substance. Human bodies and strange, alien organs could be seen under its skin—a skin that rippled and shone in the dim light. It didn't seem to have anything that could be described as a face, but there were two dark circles near the top of the thing that made Calder think of eyes.

Tentacles waved about its mass, and creatures crawled and swam through its flesh. Every now and then, one of the bodies inside it would thrash about and then go still. They floated in some kind of substance that seemed to be dissolving their flesh, some of them obviously still alive in there.

"Jesus fucking Christ," Calder breathed.

The four of them stood, their heads pounding, their stomachs threatening to spew bile out their mouths, and their eyes unable to comprehend what they were seeing. Soon a sound came into their heads that could only have been described as laughter. A strange, inhuman, wretched sound that made Calder's heart skip a beat.

You have been interesting.

The words seemed to form inside their heads, and Calder had the feeling that he only understood it through some ancient, terrifying magic. A magic that took the thing's original, alien language and chose the most suitable English equivalents.

After so long down here, you have been most interesting. But some of you are stronger than others.

"What the fuck are you?" Ekkow asked.

That dreadful laughter started again, and they all cringed as it pounded away at their brains.

There is no word to describe what we are. You are new and pitiful. Nothing but a speck in this infinite universe. We are older than you, than this place, than this world.

"How old are you?" Anna asked.

You cannot comprehend it. Of that we are sure. We have seen your kind before—when you wore nothing but the skin of animals and fought with sharpened stone. We feasted on you then, your flesh juicy but your minds primitive and uninteresting.

Visions flashed in their minds. Pictures of hunters from thousands of years ago. Ancient people fighting the creatures with nothing but spears and arrows. They watched the early humans die in unimaginable pain. A feeling overcame them, not one of horror or sadness, but of disappointment.

Your species was uninteresting. But now, there is more to you. We have been entertained. We wanted you to see us. But already your minds are starting to break.

Calder felt blood, hot and sticky, leaking from his ears and his nose. Ekkow collapsed to his knees, a cry of anguish escaping his lips. Billy followed suit. Only Anna remained standing, fighting desperately against the pounding in her head.

A shame. We will find more. The one who stands is interesting. More than the ones who fall. So much pain in your heads, so much that we can feast on. We have learned much. We shall learn more.

Calder could stand it no longer. His weapon clattered to the floor and he collapsed onto all fours. Blood poured from his nostrils. He could feel his mind melting in his skull. He screamed. Beside him, Ekkow and Billy writhed on the floor, crying out in agony.

"Hey, fuck head!" came a shout from behind the creature.

Anna looked up, seeing Priya standing on the balcony behind the thing, a pistol in her hand. She started to fire, and the throbbing in Anna's head eased. Seizing her chance, Anna lined the Molotovs along the floor and lit all of them.

It didn't take long for Priya to run out of ammunition, and the creature started to laugh again.

Your weapons are nothing. We come from the depths of the great black. We come from the cold and ice and the hostile. Your weapons are no better than sharpened stone.

"Yeah, well try this on for size, arsehole!" Anna shouted and started throwing the Molotovs at the creature.

The first hit it in the middle, the bottle bursting against its flesh, spreading burning alcohol across its body. The thing started to scream almost immediately, its flesh catching fire like tissue paper, the flames racing across it.

As the other Molotovs hit it, it became engulfed in flame. Its scream became louder, a hideous cry of inhuman anguish that ripped through their heads.

Anna was screaming something, but she didn't know what, as she tried to drag the men to their feet. Eventually, Calder came to his senses, grabbed his weapon, and stood.

He saw the smaller creatures trying to extinguish the flames, and raised his weapon when he saw Priya running past the hulking monstrosity. He put two rounds into something that made a grab for her as she sped past. It wasn't long before she was at his side, trying to help him up.

"Get Ekkow," he said, waving her off.

He fired another couple of rounds at some of the things crawling about on the flaming mass, trying to stop them from putting out the flames. One of the thing's thrashing tentacles hit the glass dome, and a crack immediately spread across it.

"Fuck. We need to move!" Calder shouted.

Ekkow was standing, Priya at his side. Anna heaved Billy up, Calder coming to her aid, and they started to move. They burst through the doors and started to run, slowly at first, clumsily, but then slowly picking up speed as the thing lost its influence over their minds.

Around them, the walls bent and splintered as the black tentacles thrashed in pain. They dodged and ducked as pieces of metal and bits of wood flew through the air around their heads. A creature stumbled into view in front of them. Ekkow raised his weapon and emptied his magazine into it.

The creature screamed and spasmed under the volley of fire, falling to the floor in pain, allowing Ekkow to jump over it as they ran.

"Almost there!" Calder shouted, glancing over his shoulder.

A wall of black, gelatinous ooze was advancing toward them, and it was then he noticed that the thrashing had stopped. He knew immediately that the glass dome must have broken and put out the flames.

"Go faster!" he screamed as they came to the bay.

By some miracle, there was already a sub in the water, and Billy, Anna, and Priya sprinted toward it as Calder and Ekkow closed the big metal door behind them. They spun the hatch wheel to seal the door.

"That should buy us some time, bruv," Ekkow said.

"But not enough," Calder said.

Calder looked around desperately for something that could work, his eyes settling on the barrels of fuel in the corner of the bay. Ekkow followed his gaze, a smile forming on his lips.

"Let's blow the fucker to Hell."

The two ex-soldiers ran toward the fuel dump. Billy stopped heading for the submarine when he saw what they were doing. He started toward them. Priya saw him go and followed, meaning to pull him with her. Anna stopped as she was halfway into the hatch.

"What are you doing?" Billy screamed. "Let's just leave!"

"Can't," Calder said, tearing his shirt off and cutting it into strips while Ekkow took the caps off of the barrels.

"We can use this to create a suitable fuse!" Ekkow said, lifting a small jerry can full of fuel up, as Calder stuffed trails of his shirt into the barrels.

"I'm afraid I can't let you do that," Billy said.

"What?" Calder asked, turning to Billy.

He realised with horror that the man's eyes were entirely black, and stood dumbstruck as his skin started to fall off of his body in wet, bloody chunks, revealing the translucent black substance beneath.

33

As the thing lifted its clawed arm to strike, the terrible laughter started again.

Calder tried to get his arms and legs to move, calling on all his training to get out the way. But it was no use. He was too tired, his mind too ravaged, his muscles too worn out. He was going to die, he realised, watching the arm come toward him with a grim fascination.

And that's when he heard Priya's scream. She barrelled into the Billy creature from out of nowhere, clawing at it with her hands. It was all Calder needed. He grabbed the jerry can from Ekkow, yelling at Priya to move.

The Billy thing lashed out, sending Priya sailing across the submarine bay. She hit the floor with a dull *thunk*, as Calder yelled out in fury. He splashed the creature with gasoline and kicked it backward, away from the fuel.

Ekkow struck his lighter and flung it at the thing, which immediately caught fire. It began to scream and thrash, running away from the two men and straight into the bulkhead at the other end of the bay.

There was no time to celebrate, as a banging sound came from the big metal door. The big creature was trying to get in. Ekkow and Calder moved fast, soaking the rags in petrol, and leaving a trail of the stuff from the barrels to the sub.

Anna was by Priya's side, tears streaming down her face. Blood soaked the floor and Anna's clothes.

"I've got her. Get in the sub," Ekkow said gently, taking the woman into his arms and walking her to the submarine.

"Anna, toss me the lighter!" Calder called before she had lowered herself inside.

She threw it to him as the banging on the door intensified. The whole bay was shaking with each hit, and a dreadful pressure had started to build inside Calder's head. The Billy creature still screamed and thrashed in the corner.

Calder ignored it all and climbed onto the top of the submarine. He struck the lighter, chucking it into the fuel trail, waiting just long enough to make sure it was lit, before slamming the hatch closed and sealing it.

"Go go go!" he shouted to Ekkow, who was at the controls.

Ekkow had already completed the set-up process and dove under the water. Outside, the flames reached the barrels, lighting the torn rags just as the metal door burst open and the black creature started flowing into the submarine bay.

The flame travelled up the rags and hit the fuel. The result was a massive explosion of heat and fire that hit the creature as it was coming it, igniting it. It thrashed and screamed and cried as the flames ripped through its flesh.

Inside the submarine, they all felt the shockwave of the explosion as it went through the water. Ekkow briefly lost control as the craft was tossed about in the current. Calder hit his head against the bulkhead, and Anna cried out in alarm. Finally, Ekkow regained control and aimed the sub toward the surface.

"Calder, help her," Anna said, cradling Priya's head in her arms.

Calder moved up to her. Blood was everywhere, soaked into her clothes, all over the floor, all over Anna. He tried to locate the source and found it pretty quickly. There was a huge gash in the woman's midriff, exposing her internal organs.

"Get... thi... news..." she rasped, blood burbling up out of her mouth, pushing something into Anna's hand.

Anna was nodding and trying to soothe her, telling her it would be fine. She was sobbing hard, blood, snot, and tears coating her face. Calder held Priya's hand, knowing there was nothing he could do.

It wasn't long before she was dead. Anna let out a terrible cry of anguish, pulling Priya's head toward her chest and hugging it.

Her shoulders shook as she sobbed. Ekkow glanced over his shoulder, a look of deep sadness on his face.

Calder let her cry. He sat next to her, tears stinging his own face as she did. No one spoke. They just sat in silence and wept.

34

"What the hell happened down there?" Richie asked.

Anna had come out first, covered in blood. She stood off to the side, something clutched in her bloodied hands.

Calder and Ekkow were pulling Priya's body out of the submarine. They laid her on the ground, Ekkow shrugging out of his shirt and laying it over the body. Richie felt bile rise in his throat at the brief glimpse of the mutilated corpse.

"You wouldn't believe me if I told you," Calder said.

Anna looked down at the thing in her hand. She found a part of her shirt that wasn't blood-soaked and wiped it.

"Here," she said, handing over a phone to Richie. "I think Priya filmed it. Everything you need to know about what happened down there."

Calder felt a wave of relief pass over him. There was evidence. They wouldn't have to explain everything to people who would think they were insane. Then he heard it, the unmistakable sound of a helicopter's rotor blades approaching.

He looked up to see a black military chopper land. One man in a suit jumped out of it and started toward the four of them.

"Who the fuck is that?" Ekkow asked.

"No idea," Richie said, bewildered.

The man that approached them was a black man who looked to be in his fifties, bald, with a big moustache. He was tall and impeccably dressed in a well-tailored grey suit. His dark-brown eyes took in the scene with practiced professionalism, finally coming to rest on Calder.

"I take it you're in charge?" the man asked.

"What's it to you, mate?" Calder spat.

"My name is Vernon Brooks. Word reached me about what I think you faced down there." He took the phone from Richie and fiddled with it for a bit.

"You know what was down there?" Anna asked, stepping forward.

Brooks remained silent as he watched the video. Finally, he looked up.

"You three need to come with me. I can help."

Calder looked at the other two. Ekkow nodded; Anna shrugged.

"Richie, I want you to take care of Priya. It looks like we have somewhere to be."

"I promise I'll look after her, Axel," he said and watched as the three of them followed Brooks to the helicopter.

"What the fuck is going on?" Anna asked through the headset as the copter took off.

Brooks looked at each of them in turn. "If I'm right, you three are the first ones in over 70 years to face something from out of this world and survive. I need to know how."

"Why?" Ekkow asked.

"Because I think there are more out there. I'll explain it all when we get to base. There's drinks and snacks in that cooler. Get some rest. You're going to need it."

As Ekkow passed candy bars and bottles of water around, Calder sat back in his seat. He watched the ocean pass beneath him. The sun was starting to rise on the horizon, and the steady rhythm of the rotor blades had a soothing quality to it.

He knew he had more nightmares in his future. But for now, he could slip into a dreamless, fatigue-driven sleep.

THE END

CHECK OUT OTHER GREAT DEEP SEA THRILLERS

THE BREACH
by Edward J. McFadden III

A Category 4 hurricane punched a quarter mile hole in Fire Island, exposing the Great South Bay to the ferocity of the Atlantic Ocean, and the current pulled something terrible through the new breach. A monstrosity of the past mixed with the present has been disturbed and it's found its way into the sheltered waters of Long Island's southern sea.

Nate Tanner lives in Stones Throw, Long Island. A disgraced SCPD detective lieutenant put out to pasture in the marine division because of his Navy background and experience with aquatic crime scenes, Tanner is assigned to hunt the creeper in the bay. But he and his team soon discover they're the ones being hunted.

INFESTATION
by William Meikle

It was supposed to be a simple mission. A suspected Russian spy boat is in trouble in Canadian waters. Investigate and report are the orders.

But when Captain John Banks and his squad arrive, it is to find an empty vessel, and a scene of bloody mayhem.

Soon they are in a fight for their lives, for there are things in the icy seas off Baffin Island, scuttling, hungry things with a taste for human flesh.

They are swarming. And they are growing.

"Scotland's best Horror writer" - Ginger Nuts of Horror

"The premier storyteller of our time." - Famous Monsters of Filmland

CHECK OUT OTHER GREAT DEEP SEA THRILLERS

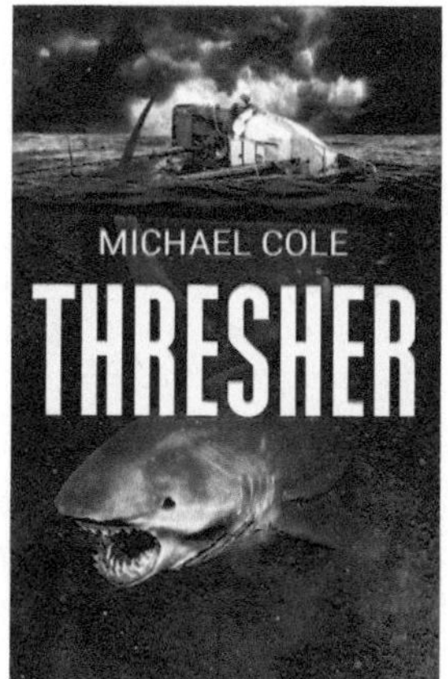

THRESHER
by Michael Cole

In the aftermath of a hurricane, a series of strange events plague the coastal waters off Florida. People go into the water and never return. Corpses of killer whales drift ashore, ravaged from enormous bite marks. A fishing trawler is found adrift, with a mysterious gash in its hull.

Transferred to the coastal town of Merit, police officer Leonard Riker uncovers the horrible reality of an enormous Thresher shark lurking off the coast. Forty feet in length, it has taken a territorial claim to the waters near the town harbor. Armed with three-inch teeth, a scythe-like caudal fin, and unmatched aggression, the beast seeks to kill anything sharing the waters.

THE GUILLOTINE
by Lucas Pederson

1,000 feet under the surface, Prehistoric Anthropologist, Ash Barrington, and his team are in the midst of a great archeological dig at the bottom of Lake Superior where they find a treasure trove of bones. Bones of dinosaurs that aren't supposed to be in this particular region. In their underwater facility, Infinity Moon, Ash and his team soon discover a series of underground tunnels. Upon exploring, they accidentally open an ice pocket, thawing the prehistoric creature trapped inside. Soon they are being attacked, the facility falling apart around them, by what Ash knows is a dunkleosteus and all those bones were from its prey. Now...Ash and his team are the prey and the creature will stop at nothing to get to them.